A NIGHT,
A SECRET…
A CHILD

A NIGHT, A SECRET... A CHILD

BY

MIRANDA LEE

First published in Great Britain 2010
Large Print edition 2010
Harlequin Mills & Boon Limited,
Eton House, 18-24 Paradise Road,
Richmond, Surrey TW9 1SR

© Miranda Lee 2010

ISBN: 978 0 263 21252 5

Harlequin Mills & Boon policy is to use papers that are
natural, renewable and recyclable products and made
from wood grown in sustainable forests. The logging and
manufacturing process conform to the legal environmental
regulations of the country of origin.

Printed and bound in Great Britain
by CPI Antony Rowe, Chippenham, Wiltshire

CHAPTER ONE

NICOLAS moved with uncharacteristic slowness as he alighted the cab outside his apartment building. He felt dog-tired and strangely lacking in the buzz that finding and promoting an exciting new talent usually brought him.

Admittedly, standing in the wings of a stage and watching someone else perform had never given him the same adrenalin rush as being out there himself. But being the man behind a successful star or show had come a close second this past decade.

Tonight, however, his pulse rate hadn't risen when his latest musical protégée had brought the highly discerning New York audience to its feet more than once. He was happy for her. Of course he was. She was a nice girl and a brilliant violinist. But he just hadn't felt anything like what he normally did. In truth, he hadn't given a damn.

How odd.

Maybe he was entering a midlife crisis: next year he'd turn forty. Or perhaps he was reaching burnout. Showbiz was a wearing career, both on the performers and the promoters. Lots of highs and lows. And lots of travelling.

Nicolas had grown to hate hotel rooms very quickly. That was why he'd eventually bought apartments in New York and London. His friends called him extravagant. But Nicolas knew he'd chosen well and would never lose money on his purchases. His New York apartment had already tripled in value in the six years he'd owned it. His London town house wasn't quite as spectacular an investment, but he certainly hadn't lost money.

'Everything go well tonight, Mr Dupre?' the night doorman asked as he opened the door for Nicolas. There was a note of concern in his voice. Obviously he'd seen the weariness in Nicolas's body language.

Nicolas flashed the doorman a warm smile. 'Very well, Mike. Thank you.'

The doorman nodded. 'That's good.'

Nicolas might have given him a tip if Mike would have accepted it. But Mike refused to take money from the residents, only guests and visitors. Nicolas always slipped him a card and a nice fat cheque at Christmas, claiming he would be offended if Mike refused to take his Christmas present. Nicolas suspected Mike probably gave most of the money away to someone he considered more needy than himself; he was that kind of man.

The young man on the front desk glanced up as Nicolas entered the foyer. Chad was a third-year law student who worked nights to pay his way through college. Nicolas admired anyone who worked hard and had given Chad more than a little something last Christmas as well.

'There's a letter here for you, sir,' Chad said.

'A letter?'

Nicolas frowned as he walked up to the desk. He never received mail these days. All his bills and bank statements were redirected to his accountant. If anyone wanted to contact him personally they did so by phone, text message or email.

The young man smiled. 'The mailman brought it in this afternoon after you'd left for the theatre. Have to confess we had a bit of a chuckle over it. You'll know what I mean when you see the way it's addressed.' And he handed over a bright pink envelope.

On it was written:

Mr Nicolas Dupre
c/o Broadway
New York
America

'Good Lord,' Nicolas said with a wry smile.

'Nice to be famous,' Chad said.

'I'm not all that famous.' Not nowadays. It was mainly the entertainers who were interviewed on the talk shows, not the entrepreneurs. Nicolas had had one television interview a couple of years back, after one of the musicals he'd produced had won heaps of Tony awards, but nothing since.

'It's come all the way from Australia,' Chad said, and Nicolas's heart missed a beat.

Something—some inner instinct—warned him not to turn the envelope over and look at the sender's name…. Not till he was safely alone.

'Looks like it's from a lady,' Chad went on, obviously dying to know who.

Nicolas, however, had no intention of satisfying the younger man's curiosity.

'An old fan, I imagine,' Nicolas said, and slipped the envelope inside his breast pocket. 'Someone who doesn't know I stopped performing years ago. Thank you, Chad. Good night.'

'Oh…er… Good night, sir.'

Nicolas made it into the privacy of his tenth-floor apartment before he extracted the envelope and looked at the back flap.

His stomach churned as he stared at the name of the sender. It wasn't from her. Had he honestly expected that it would be? Had he been hoping against hope that Serina had finally come to her senses and realised that she couldn't live without him?

Once he got over his dismay, the letter did, however, evoke considerable surprise and curiosity. Because it was from Serina's daughter, the child whom Nicolas had once briefly thought could be his, but wasn't. Felicity Harmon had been born ten months to the day after the last time he'd slept with Serina, and exactly nine months after her marriage to Greg Harmon.

Nicolas still had trouble accepting what Serina had done that night. It had been cruel of her to come back into his life and raise his hopes where she was concerned.

It had taken him years to get over her initial refusal to go to England with him when he'd been just twenty-one. But he'd finally come to understand and accept—or he thought he had— that her love for her family back in Rocky Creek was much stronger than her love for him. He'd stayed away from home after that, not even returning to visit his mother. Instead, a couple of times a year, he'd send his mother money to travel to whatever part of the world he was in. Why torture himself?

Serina was the one who'd eventually sought him out, several years later.

He'd imagined he was over her by then. There'd been other women, lots of them. The fact he'd never lived with one, let alone married any of them, should have told him that his heart still belonged to Serina, that heart taking off into the stratosphere when he'd spotted her in the audience as he'd been taking his curtain call that fateful night, thirteen years ago. He recalled the date very well because it was the first time he'd performed in Sydney, having stayed right away from Australia as well as Rocky Creek.

When she'd appeared at his dressing-room door afterwards, he'd been incapable of speech.

He'd taken one look into her lovely, tear-filled eyes, pulled her inside the room and locked the door behind her. They'd made love on the sofa with a hunger that had been insatiable, before sheer exhaustion had had them both falling asleep in each other's arms.

When he'd woken she'd gone, leaving him a note saying that she was sorry, but she simply hadn't been able to resist the temptation to be with him one last time. She'd begged him not to follow her home. She was marrying Greg Harmon in a few weeks and nothing he could do or say was going to change her mind. He could still recall her final argument, word for word.

'Your life is playing the piano, Nicolas. It's what you want and what you need—to perform. I could see that tonight. What we have when we're together, it's not love, Nicolas, it's something else. Something dangerous. If I give in to it, it will destroy me. You will survive without me, I know you will.'

Well, he had. Survived, that is. Though it had been touch-and-go a couple of times.

Yet it had only taken the arrival of a pink envelope from Australia to make his heart race in that crazy way it always raced when he was with Serina. He'd thought she'd felt the same way about him once. And maybe she had. Looking back, he could see she'd been as powerless to resist him physically, as he'd been her. As lovers, they'd been perfect together, right from the start. Amazing, considering they'd both been virgins.

Nicolas shook his head at the memory of that night. If he'd known what was going to happen he would never have agreed to Mrs Johnson's suggestion that Serina partner him to his graduation ball.

At that time in his life, Nicolas had had no time for girls. His only passion had been the piano.

Not that the girls weren't after him; they were. At eighteen, Nicolas had been tall and handsome, with wavy blond hair and Nordic-blue eyes, which he'd been told were sexy. There'd been any number of girls in his class and in other classes at his high school who would have gladly agreed to go with him to his grad. But Nicolas just hadn't wanted the complications that came with having a girlfriend. His focus had been all on his career back then. All he could think about was becoming the world's greatest concert pianist. He'd already won a

scholarship to go to the Conservatorium of
Music in Sydney and would be leaving to study
there in a couple of months' time. His life in
Rocky Creek—which he'd always hated—
would soon be over.

But his mother had really wanted him to go to
his graduation ball, so he'd given in to his music
teacher's suggestion and asked Serina, who was
another of Mrs Johnson's piano pupils. Nicolas
had reasoned—incorrectly as it turned out—that
because she was rather shy Serina was unlikely to
become a problem. Conversation wouldn't be difficult, either. They could always talk about music.

Imagine his surprise—and shock—when he
went to pick her up in his mother's car and a
vision of loveliness came walking through her
front door. She was wearing blue, a deep electric
blue. Her dress was strapless, its material shiny,
with a bell-shaped skirt, and her shoes were
high. Her very shapely legs seemed to go on
forever.

Up till then Nicolas had only ever seen Serina
in her school uniform, with no makeup and her
hair either in a plait or up in a pony tail.

Suddenly, with her hair down, her face made
up and her amazingly grown-up figure very

much on display, she looked much older and extremely sexy. Nicolas took one look at her and was struck by a desire he'd never felt before. He could not take his eyes off her all night. Dancing with her became both a delight and a torment.

He was in quite a frazzled state by the time they left the ball and he drove Serina home shortly after midnight. Her parents had made a condition of her going with him that he wouldn't take her on to any of the after-grad parties, which were well known for being drunken booze-ups and sex-fests. Nicolas didn't mind, since he didn't drink and wasn't into sex. Not as yet, anyway.

Suddenly, however, he wanted Serina even more than he wanted to dazzle the world with his piano playing. But he knew it was out of the question. For one thing, his date was obviously a virgin, like himself.

But just as they were approaching Rocky Creek, Serina's hand slid over and came to rest on his thigh. His eyes flew to hers and what he saw there echoed his own quite desperate need.

'Don't take me home yet,' she whispered huskily.

Nicolas needed no more encouragement,

swiftly turning his mother's car off the main road onto a narrow bush track, which he knew would bring him to a very private spot down by the creek.

And it was there that it all began. Just kisses at first, then touching and more touching. Clothes came off and before he knew it he was trying to get inside her. Her gasp of pain didn't stop him, either. By then he was beyond thought, beyond control. Only afterwards did he panic, because he hadn't used a condom.

'Your father's going to kill me if you get pregnant,' he'd groaned.

'I can't,' came her surprisingly calm reply. 'Not tonight, anyway. I've just finished my period. According to a book I read that means I'm safe.'

Nicolas breathed a huge sigh of relief.

'I'll go in to Port and buy some condoms tomorrow,' he replied, and she just stared up at him, her eyes large and dark.

'It'll be better next time,' he heard himself promise.

'I liked it this time,' she stunned him by saying. 'It was lovely. Do it to me again, Nicolas.'

And he did. More slowly the second time, watching with wonder as she came. By the time he took her home around two, Nicolas was totally obsessed with her.

Somehow, they managed to keep their teenage love affair a secret during that entire summer holiday, Nicolas sneaking out of his bedroom every night and running all the way to meet Serina down behind her house. Fortunately, her parents lived on a small farm that had lots of outbuildings where they could make love. Nicolas made Serina promise not to tell anyone about their relationship, especially not any of her girlfriends. He knew that Serina's rather old-fashioned parents would do everything to separate them if they found out what was going on. Publicly, they pretended to their small community that they were just friends, brought together by the fact that they were both pupils of the same music teacher.

It wasn't till later that they began to date openly. By then Nicolas had gone to Sydney to study and the star-crossed lovers didn't see each other all that much. When they did, however, they made the most of their time together. They would tell their respective parents that they were practising the piano together, or going to the movies, or to the beach.

But an unwanted pregnancy and a teenage marriage were not in Nicolas's plans for his immediate future, not if he was going to become the world's greatest concert pianist.

However, he'd always known that Serina was the only girl for him, that one day they would marry, and he would be the father of her children. It had seemed inconceivable to him back then that she would ever be with another man, let alone bear a child.

Yet she'd had another man's child—and that child had just written to him.

Why, for pity's sake?

Nicolas ripped open the pink envelope and out came a white sheet of paper on which was a computer-generated letter.

Dear Mr Dupre
Hi. My name is Felicity Harmon. I live in Rocky Creek and I am twelve years old. I am captain of our primary school and am helping the teachers organise an end-of-year concert to be held on Saturday afternoon, the twentieth of December this year, to raise funds for our local bushfire brigade.
We are going to have a talent quest instead

of a normal concert and need someone to act as judge for the night. It would be nice to have someone famous so that lots of people will come. You are the most famous person to have ever lived in Rocky Creek, and I thought I would write and ask you to come and be our judge. My piano teacher, Mrs Johnson, said you probably wouldn't come because you live in New York now and you don't have family here anymore. But she also said you were once good friends with my mum and you just might come, if I asked nicely. You probably don't know this but my dad was killed not that long ago. He went to help down in the terrible bushfires in Victoria last summer and a burnt-out tree fell on him. He told me the day before he died that our local bushfire brigade needed better fire-fighting equipment to keep our town safe from bushfires. A new truck would be good. But new trucks cost a lot of money.

I'm sure that if you come and be our judge we would make a lot of money. If you can come, you could stay at our house as we have a spare bedroom. Below is my email address if you think you can make it. I hope

you can. Please let me know soon, as the
concert is only three weeks away.
Yours sincerely
Felicity Harmon.
PS. I used a pink envelope because I thought
it might stand out and have a better chance
of finding you.
PPS. If it does, please come!

Please come! That was a laugh. Wild horses
couldn't keep him away.

If Greg Harmon had still been alive, Nicolas
would not even have dreamt of going back to
Rocky Creek. He would politely have declined
Felicity's undeniably touching plea, then have
posted her a large, disappointment-saving cheque.

But the carrot had been waved, hadn't it? Serina
was now a widow. How could he not return?

She'd always been his Achilles' heel. Always
driven him crazy. One day, she'd probably be the
death of him.

It was a prophetic thought…

CHAPTER TWO

SERINA stared with disbelieving eyes at her daughter. Felicity's bald announcement over breakfast that she'd secured Nicolas Dupre as the judge of her school's fund-raising talent quest had rendered her temporarily speechless.

'But how did you know where to contact him?' she finally managed to blurt out.

Felicity's impossibly smug expression reminded Serina quite fiercely of her father. Her biological father, that was, not the man who'd raised her.

'I didn't,' Felicity replied. 'I wrote him a letter and addressed it care of Broadway, New York. And he got it!'

Serina scooped in a deep breath whilst she prayed for calm.

'And?'

'I gave him my email address and he sent me a reply last night.'

'Why didn't you tell me all this last night?'

'His email didn't come till after you'd gone to bed.'

'Felicity! You know I don't like you being on the Internet after I go to bed.'

'Yeah, I know. Sorry,' she apologised without a trace of guilt in her voice.

Serina glared at her daughter. Felicity was a wilful child and far too intelligent for her own good. On top of that she was a brilliant pianist. Mrs Johnson often said she was the most talented musician she'd taught since…

Serina swallowed. This couldn't be happening to her!

'Felicity, I…'

'Mum, please don't be mad at me,' Felicity broke in. 'I had to do something or no one would've come to our talent quest except for the parents. This way lots of other people will come. We might even make enough money to buy one of those brand-new fire trucks. One which has sprinklers on top like Dad always wanted. I'm doing this for Dad, Mum. He can't do it from heaven, can he?'

What could Serina say to that? Nothing, really. Felicity had adored Greg, had been devastated by his death. She'd been the apple of Greg's eye and he'd never known the truth about his daughter's parentage. Serina had managed to keep her guilty secret from everyone, even Nicolas himself, who'd broached the subject of his possible paternity when he'd returned briefly to Rocky Creek a decade ago to attend his mother's funeral.

Fate—and genetics—had helped her with her deception and denials. First, she'd carried her baby for ten months, something that happened occasionally on the maternal side of her family. Her great aunt had had a couple of ten-month pregnancies. On top of that, her daughter had been born with dark hair and eyes, the same as herself and Greg, not with Nicolas's fair colouring. Also, Felicity had been little more than a baby at the time of Mrs Dupre's death, so she hadn't started taking piano lessons. There was no evidence of her then having taken after Nicolas, nothing at all to make him suspicious. Even now, everyone in Rocky Creek thought Felicity had inherited her musical talent from her. Given that her relationship with Nicolas had broken up years before, this was only logical. Who would imagine that the very respectable

Serina Harmon would have gone to Sydney and made mad passionate love with her ex-boyfriend a mere month before her wedding? It was unthinkable!

But then, Nicolas had always made her to do the unthinkable.

She would have done anything for him at one stage. Anything except abandon her family when they'd most needed her.

How could she have gone to England with him after her father's stroke? It had been impossible. Nicolas had been stunned when she'd refused, then furious. He'd claimed she didn't love him enough.

But she had. Too much. In a way, the power of her love for Nicolas had terrified the life out of her. She wasn't herself when she was with him. She became his slave, a nothing person with no will of her own. He only had to take her in his arms and she was reduced to being a robot, incapable of saying no to him.

Knowing this, she'd made her initial stand against him over the phone. Nicolas had just won a concerto competition in Sydney and the prize would take him to England to study and perform. He'd rung her immediately and insisted she accompany him, though there'd not been an offer of marriage, she'd noted. She'd be his travelling companion as well as his personal assistant—and, most of all, his extremely accommodating love slave.

'I can't go with you, Nicolas,' she'd choked out even as the tears had run down her cheeks. 'Not now. I have to stay in Rocky Creek and help run the family business. There's no one else, only me.' She'd had no brothers or sisters to help, having been an only child. And her mother had had to stay home and nurse her father.

Nicolas had raged at her for ages—raged and argued. But she'd stayed firm that time. Much easier with him so far away. When he'd threatened to return to Rocky Creek to persuade her, she'd claimed he would be wasting his time, adding the desperate lie that she was sick to death of their long-distance relationship anyway. In truth, since he'd gone to Sydney to study, she only saw him on the odd weekend when he came home, and during holidays. He sometimes didn't even come home for those. More than once he'd gone away to a music camp.

'I want a normal boyfriend,' Serina had wailed. 'One who isn't obsessed with music. And one who lives in Rocky Creek! Greg Harmon's always asking me out,' she'd added quite truthfully.

'Greg Harmon! He's old enough to be your father!'

'No, he's not.' Greg did look older than he was. But actually he was only in his late twenties, a local fellow who worked as a teacher in nearby Wauchope High School, where both Serina and Nicolas had studied. Although she had never actually been in any of Greg's classes—he taught agriculture and woodwork—she'd always known he fancied her.

He'd started asking her out the moment she'd graduated from school.

'He's a very nice man,' Serina had snapped defensively. 'And very good-looking. Next time he asks me out, I'm going to say yes.'

It had almost been a relief when Nicolas had stormed off to England by himself. But then she'd never heard from him again: no letters or phone calls begging her forgiveness; nothing but a bitter silence.

Serina had taken a long time to get over Nicolas. But, in the end, sheer loneliness had forced her into saying yes to Greg's persistent requests to take her out. In the back of her mind,

however, she'd always believed Nicolas would
return one day to claim her. So she didn't sleep
with Greg at first, or accept any of his regular
proposals of marriage.

But as time went by and Nicolas didn't return
to Rocky Creek, Serina let Greg put an engagement ring on her finger. And take her to bed,
after which she'd cried and cried. Not because
it was awful. Greg turned out to be a tender
and considerate lover. But because he wasn't
Nicolas.

Still, in time, she managed to push Nicolas
right to the back of her mind and began making
concrete plans for her wedding to Greg.
Although not ecstatically happy, Serina was rea-
sonably content with her life. She was loved by
her fiancé, family and friends, and respected in
the community. She was also finding great satisfaction in expanding the family's lumber yard
into a more extensive building supply business,
local demand increasing as Rocky Creek gradually became a very desirable 'tree-change' destination for retirees and tired city dwellers.

If only she hadn't made that fateful trip to
Sydney in search of the right wedding dress...
If only she hadn't seen Nicolas's interview on

television in her hotel room... If only she'd stayed away from his performance that night at the Opera House...

Serina glanced across the breakfast table at her daughter and wondered, not for the first time, if she'd done the right thing, passing Felicity off as Greg's daughter. It hadn't been a deliberate act on her part. By the time she'd realised she was pregnant, the wedding was upon her and she hadn't had the heart to hurt Greg as she knew the truth would have hurt him. And hurt everyone else: her parents, his parents, their friends.

Life in a small country town was not as simple as people sometimes thought.

No, I made the right decision, she accepted philosophically, *the only decision.*

Greg was a devoted husband and father and I had a good life with him, a nice, peaceful life. I still lead a nice, peaceful life.

But that peace was about to be broken. Big-time.

Fear clutched at her stomach. Fear of what might happen when she saw Nicolas again—this time without the moral protection of a husband in her life. She still hadn't forgotten how she'd felt when she'd seen him at his mother's funeral. That had been ten years ago, when she'd been twenty-seven and Nicolas an incredibly dashing thirty. Greg had insisted they both attend, Mrs Dupre having been a well-loved member in their small community. They'd taken Felicity with them. She'd been around two at the time. It was at the wake that Nicolas had cornered her, getting her alone after Greg had carried their daughter outside to play for a while.

Nicolas had been cold to her, as cold as ice.

She hadn't felt cold, however. Even whilst he'd questioned her about Felicity's birth date in the most chilling and contemptuous fashion, she'd burned with a desire that she'd found both disturbing and despicable. It still upset her to think of what might have happened if Nicolas had made any kind of pass at her.

Fortunately, he hadn't.

But who knew what he might do now that she was a widow. Had Felicity told him Greg was dead? It seemed likely that she had.

'Do you have a copy of the letter you sent Mr Dupre?' she asked her daughter somewhat stiffly.

Felicity looked pained. 'Oh, Mum, that's private!'

'I want to see it, Felicity. And the email he sent back to you.'

Felicity pouted and stayed right where she was.

Serina rose from her chair, her expression uncompromising. 'Let's go, madam.'

Serina found her daughter's letter very touching, till she got to the part where Felicity offered Nicolas accommodation at their house.

'He can't stay here!' she blurted out before she could get control of herself.

'Why not?' Felicity demanded to know with the indignation—and innocence—of youth.

'Because.'

'Because why?' her daughter persisted.

'Because you don't ask virtual strangers to stay in your home,' she answered in desperation.

'But he's not a stranger. He lived here in Rocky Creek for years and years. Mrs Johnson said you were very good friends. She said you dated for a while.'

'Only very casually,' Serina lied. 'And, as I said, that was nearly twenty years ago. I have no idea what kind of man Nicolas Dupre might have become in the meantime. For all I know he could be a drunk, or a drug addict!'

Felicity looked at her as though she were insane.

'Mum, I think you've totally lost it. But you don't
have to worry. Mr Dupre refused my offer to stay
with us. Here! Why don't you read his email and
then you won't say such silly things.'

Felicity did a couple of clicks with her mouse
and brought up the email from Nicolas. Serina
read it.

Dear Felicity
Thank you for your lovely letter. I was sad-
dened to hear of the tragic death of your fa-
ther and send my deepest condolences to you
and your mother. I have fond memories of
Rocky Creek and would be glad to help you
with your fund-raising project. You sound
like a very intelligent and enterprising young
lady of whom I'm sure your mother is very
proud. Consequently, I would be honoured to
be the judge for your talent quest.
Unfortunately, I have business engagements
in New York and London for the next fort-
night and cannot arrive in Sydney till the
day before your concert. Thank you for your
kind offer of a room but I would prefer to
arrange my own accommodation in Port
Macquarie. I will contact you by phone as

soon as I arrive there, at which time you can explain where and when you want me to be the following day. Please confirm this arrangement by return email and include your home phone number.

My regards to your mother and Mrs Johnson. I am looking forward to meeting up with them both once again.

All the best, Nicolas Dupre.

Serina didn't know what to say. The email was extremely polite. Too polite, in fact, and a bit pompous. It didn't sound at all like Nicolas.

Maybe what she'd said to Felicity was right in a way. She didn't know him anymore. The passing years might have changed him from the impassioned and rather angry young man he'd once been into something entirely different. Someone calm and mature and yes…kind. Maybe he was coming all this way out of kindness. Maybe it had nothing to do with her being a widow now, nothing to do with her at all! Nicolas was just responding to the heartfelt request of a young girl whose father had been tragically killed.

Serina tried to embrace this possibility but she

simply couldn't. She knew, in her heart of hearts, that his coming back to Rocky Creek had nothing to do with kindness. It was all about her.

Not that she believed Nicolas was still in love with her. He'd made his contempt quite clear at his mother's funeral. But maybe he'd spotted the hunger in her eyes. Maybe his plan was to take full advantage of that hunger, to do to her what she'd once done to him: indulge in a wild one-night stand, then dump her in the morning.

A shiver ran down Serina's spine, a highly disturbing, cruelly seductive shiver.

Please, don't let that be his plan. Let him be coming back for something else. To visit his mother's grave perhaps. Don't let me be his underlying motive, or his prey. Don't let him be looking for sexual revenge. Because this time, I have nowhere to run to, and no one to hide behind...

CHAPTER THREE

NICOLAS could have hired a car in Sydney and driven to Port Macquarie. But that was a five- to six-hour drive, maybe longer, given that his early morning arrival at Mascot would mean he would hit peak hour traffic going through the city. He'd done just that when he'd returned to Rocky Creek for his mother's funeral and regretted it. He'd regretted also hiring a stupid sports car, which hadn't coped too well with the not-so-wonderful roads up that way.

This time, he booked a connecting flight to Port Macquarie that left Sydney at 8:00 am and only took fifty-five minutes. Once there, he planned to take a taxi to his accommodation where the four-wheel-drive vehicle he'd already hired would be waiting for him. He hadn't wanted the bother of picking it up at the airport. Experience had taught him that doing so could be a very time-consuming operation. Having made the decision to come, Nicolas knew that he couldn't bear the thought of anything delaying his arrival in Rocky Creek. The weariness he'd been feeling the night Felicity's letter had arrived was long gone, replaced by the kind of excitement he used to feel just before going on the stage to perform.

Everything went according to plan. The flight from London set down at Mascot only a few minutes late and the connecting flight to Port Macquarie left right on time. Nicolas stepped out onto the tarmac at Port Macquarie airport right on nine. Fifteen minutes later, he and his luggage were speeding towards the centre of town.

'Port's grown since I was last here,' he remarked as he glanced around. 'But it has been nearly twenty years.'

'Crikey, mate,' the taxi driver replied. 'You'll be lucky to recognise anything.'

Not true, however. The town centre hadn't changed all that much, Nicolas thought as they drove down the main street. The rectangular layout was basically the same, the streets straight and wide, with parking at the curb sides and in the middle. The old picture theatre was still there on the corner and the pub across the road. But

the evidence of a tourism explosion was everywhere, with all the high-rise apartment buildings
and the upsurge in restaurants and cafés.

And of course, the tourists themselves were
there in full force. Summer had arrived in
Australia and with it the hot weather that sent
people flocking to seaside towns. Nicolas was
already feeling a little sticky. He'd be glad to
have a shower and change into something cooler
than the suit, shirt and tie he was currently
wearing.

The taxi turned right at the end of the main
street and headed up the hill to where Nicolas's
choice of accommodation was located, a relatively new boutique apartment block that was
several storeys high and made the most of its
position overlooking Town Beach. Nicolas had
found it on one of the many travel Web sites
available and booked one of the apartments
from his home in London a couple of nights
back.

Although book-in time was officially not till
2:00 pm, Nicolas was soon given his keys. The
apartment he'd chosen had not been occupied the
previous night. Not surprising, given the hefty
price tag and the fact that last night was a

Thursday. Added to this was the fact that he'd taken it for a full week.

Nicolas was suitably impressed when he let himself in and walked around, inspecting what his two grand had bought him. There was a spacious living room that combined the sitting and dining areas and opened out onto an equally large, sea-facing balcony, with a barbeque, outdoor furniture and a hot tub. The bedroom was five-star, the bed king-sized, as was the plasma television screen built into the wall opposite the foot of the bed. The en suite bathroom was total luxury with gold taps, crystal light fittings and a spa bath fit for two. The kitchen was superbly appointed with black granite countertops and stainless steel appliances.

Nicolas noted the complimentary bottles of wine in the fridge. Not just champagne, but Chardonnay and Chablis. There were also a couple of bottles of fine Hunter Valley reds resting in the stainless steel wine rack. A bowl of fresh fruit sat on the coffee table and a box of chocolates, too.

Serina had a sweet tooth, he recalled.

Serina…

How would she react to him this time? he wondered as he unzipped the first of his two cases and began to unpack.

She'd been extremely tense when he'd confronted her after his mother's funeral. Fearful, he suspected, that he might say something to her husband. No doubt she'd never confessed to Greg that she'd slept with him not long before their wedding.

His own mood had been vicious. Grief combined with jealousy had not made him ready to be kind, or forgiving. He'd questioned Serina mercilessly about her daughter's parentage, even though his eyes had already told him that the pretty little dark-haired, dark-eyed child wasn't his.

And all the time they were talking together, he'd been fiercely erect. Wanting her. Loving her. Hating her.

She'd looked even more beautiful than he remembered. Black became her. There again, just about any colour suited Serina, with her dark hair and eyes, and lovely olive skin. Having a child had enhanced rather than spoilt her figure. Her curves were the curves of a woman in her prime. She'd looked luscious, and as sexy as ever.

It had killed him to watch her leave the wake with another man, to see the proprietorial way Greg had taken her arm and led her away.

Nicolas hadn't slept a wink that night. He'd tossed and turned, picturing Serina in her marital bed, in her husband's arms, under her husband's body.

The next morning, a grim-faced Nicolas had given instructions to his mother's solicitor to dispose of the house and all its contents, and forward the proceeds to his bank in London. By noon he'd left Rocky Creek, vowing never to return.

Yet here he was, doing just that.

Of course, he'd never imagined that the extremely healthy-looking Greg Harmon would die so young. Or that Serina's daughter would write to him and practically beg him to come back to Rocky Creek.

Nicolas wondered what Serina felt about Felicity doing that? Would she have been annoyed? Angry? It had been rather bold of the girl to write to him like that. He suspected it had been done without her mother's permission.

The fact there'd been no email from Serina herself had been telling, he thought. The principal of Rocky Creek Primary school had emailed him, checking that his offer was for real, but nothing, however, from Felicity's mother.

Perhaps her silence meant indifference. But he doubted it.

Serina could never be indifferent to him, just as he could never be indifferent to her.

As Nicolas carried his toilet bag into the bathroom, he made another vow. He wasn't going to leave Australia this time till he knew for certain how Serina felt about him and how he felt about her. He was not going to live the rest of his life pining for what might have been, or what might be in the future.

He'd booked this apartment for a full week. Long enough, he imagined, to have all his questions answered...

CHAPTER FOUR

SERINA found it impossible to concentrate at work that Friday morning. All she could think about was the fact that Nicolas was on his way here right at this moment; that soon, he would reach Port Macquarie and call, not Felicity or Fred Tarleton, Felicity's school's principal, but her own sorry self.

Felicity, the precocious child, had informed her of these new arrangements late last night, explaining that she'd given Nicolas her mobile number to contact when he arrived at Port Macquarie, as everyone at the school would be tied up all day, getting the school hall ready for the concert the following evening. Everything had to be perfect for their famous visiting judge.

There had been no use protesting. Felicity was as stubborn as a mule. And Nicolas, it seemed, was uncontactable at that hour, having already boarded his plane in London for the flight to

Sydney. It hadn't occurred to Serina till she'd arrived at work this morning that he probably had one of those fandangled new phones that received emails, even on planes. Serina had never been overly keen on technology and whilst she used a computer at work and carried a basic mobile phone with her, she didn't have a PC of her own at home and wasn't at all enamoured with the Internet.

Felicity, however, like most modern children, was a real computer buff and could make her way around the worldwide web with ridiculous ease. Over the past fortnight she'd regaled Serina with scads of information about Nicolas that she'd found on the Internet, from his earliest concert playing days right up to the successes he'd had as a theatrical entrepreneur, including that of his latest musical protégée, a young Japanese violinist called Junko Hoshino who was as beautiful as she was talented. Several gossip columnists had them being an item already. It seemed Nicolas had somewhat of a reputation as a ladies' man, a fact that didn't surprise.

Serina already knew quite a bit about Nicolas's life over the past decade. There'd been a segment on *60 Minutes* a couple of years ago back that was like a mini *This is Your Life*, highlighting the accident that had ended his piano playing career, then praising him for the way he'd put such a tragedy behind him and forged a new career in show business.

It had made difficult viewing with Greg by her side on the lounge. She'd wanted to tape the segment and watch it over and over—watch him over and over—but hadn't dared. Greg knew she'd once dated Nicolas, though she'd always downplayed their relationship, claiming she hadn't been unhappy when he left Australia to pursue his career. Later that night, when Greg had wanted sex, however, she'd turned him down, because she knew she simply could not bear to make love with her husband with the memory of Nicolas so fresh in her mind.

He was very fresh in her mind again today, not just because he was on his way to Rocky Creek but because of what she'd watched on Felicity's computer last night. That incorrigible child had found an old video of him on a social networking site showing him playing one of Chopin's polonaises at the Royal Albert Hall.

'You have to come and look at this, Mum,' she'd insisted.

Serina had, very reluctantly at first. But then with total concentration on the screen.

No one, in Serina's opinion, played the piano quite like Nicolas. She had no doubt that lots of concert pianists—past and present—were more technically brilliant. But none possessed his passion, his panache, or his blatant sex appeal.

Women had swooned over him when he played. She certainly had that fateful night. His performance—even on this grainy video—sent sexual shivers running down her spine.

'Wasn't he an incredible pianist, Mum?' Felicity had raved.

'Yes,' Serina had agreed huskily, her tongue thick in her throat.

'And to think he can't play anymore! I cried when I read about his hands being burned like that. But it was very brave of him to do what he did, wasn't it?'

'Yes,' Serina had agreed again, this time in a more composed voice. 'Very brave.'

Which it had been. Apparently, he'd been walking along a street in central London very late one night—not long after his mother died—

when a passing car had careered out of control on a corner, hit a brick wall and burst into flames. The driver—a woman—had been knocked unconscious. Nicolas had raced over and dragged her out. He'd just pulled her clear when he'd heard the baby crying. It had taken him some considerable time to undo the seat belt and extricate the baby from its capsule in the backseat, during which time his hands had been burned, his left hand so badly that his left thumb had had to eventually be amputated.

Serina had cried, too, when she'd first heard about Nicolas's burnt hand. It had been widely covered in the news at the time. Greg had found her weeping over it in her bedroom, but thought she was crying over her inability to conceive another child. She'd let him think that. For how could she explain her distress over Nicolas's accident?

She'd felt guilty, though. She'd felt guilty a lot during her marriage. That was the one thing that Greg's death had released her from. Feeling guilty.

There was no guilt in Serina today. The guilt had been replaced by the most excruciating nervous tension.

Her eyes kept going to the clock on the wall. Only ten-fifteen. If he was driving, Nicolas couldn't possibly be in Port yet. His plane didn't touch down in Mascot till six-thirty this morning. By the time he got through customs and rented a car he would have hit peak hour traffic in Sydney. It would take him till well after nine to get out of the city and onto the freeway. Once you included a couple of stops for food and nature calling, plus all the delays caused by the road works around Bulahdelah and Taree, his estimated time of arrival would be around three or four this afternoon.

But, of course, he might not be driving up. He might have taken a connecting flight. She herself had never flown anywhere from Port. When she went to Sydney by herself that one time, she'd taken the train from Wauchope. Then, after her marriage to Greg, on the few occasions they'd gone to Sydney, they'd driven down. But she knew there was a flight from Sydney that got in around ten. If it was on time, it would take Nicolas about half an hour to collect his luggage and get to wherever he was staying in Port. Which meant she could expect a call anytime now.

Serina had just finished this mental calculation

when her phone rang. Not her work phone but her mobile.

'That'll be him!' Allie called out from the reception desk.

'If it is then he couldn't have driven,' Serina said.

'Of course not!' Emma said impatiently from her nearby desk. 'A man like that. He wouldn't drive all this way when he could fly.'

Both the girls who worked with Serina in the office knew everything about Nicolas's visit—and the man himself—courtesy of Felicity dropping by every second morning to give them an update, including this morning. Fortunately, neither of the girls were old enough to have been at high school with either Serina or Nicolas, so they believed everything Serina told them about her relationship with the famous entrepreneur.

Nonetheless, being typical females, they were quick to suggest that her 'just good friends' status with the famous Nicolas Dupre might develop into something more once he got to see her again. Both Allie and Emma were openly admiring of their boss's looks and style, and had recently begun to try to matchmake her with every single man in Rocky Creek. Unfortunately—or perhaps fortunately—there weren't too many local men around Serina's age who weren't already married, or Mumma's boys, or simply too unattractive for words.

In truth, Serina had no interest in getting married again. Or even in dating.

But Allie and Emma didn't believe her.

'For pity's sake, Serina,' Allie snapped. 'Will you stop staring at that darned phone and just answer it!'

Serina winced as she swept up her phone from where it was vibrating all over her desktop.

'Hello?' she croaked out.

'Serina? Is that you?'

It was Nicolas. His voice was extremely memorable, being rich and deep and as smooth as melted chocolate.

Serina cleared the lump in her throat. 'Yes, yes, it's me, Nicolas,' she went on, hopefully sounding more like the calm, confident woman she usually was around the office. 'So where are you?'

'In Port Macquarie.'

'Oh. You flew, then. So where are you staying?'

'The Blue Horizon Apartments.'

The newest and most luxurious in Port. Trust Nicolas to choose the best. That segment she'd seen on TV had been filmed in his New York apartment, which was like a show home and probably worth millions.

'Did you have a good flight from London?' she said, well aware of Allie and Emma listening in.

'Great. I slept all the way.'

Which was more than could be said for herself last night.

'I always take a sleeping tablet on overnight flights,' he added. 'And I travel first class, which helps.'

'I'm sure it does.'

Serina grimaced. Did that sound waspish? She hoped it didn't, because that betrayed emotion and she was determined to remain cool around Nicolas. On the surface, anyway. She'd vowed during the long hours she'd lain awake last night that she was not going to let him get to her in any way.

But that was last night and this was now. Serina had an awful feeling that any vows she'd made where Nicolas was concerned would not stand up once they were face-to-face. Bad enough just talking to him. Her heartbeat had already doubled and her hand—the one clutching the phone—felt decidedly clammy.

Of course it was hot today. The forecast was for thirty-six degrees. But their office was air-conditioned. There was no reason for her to have sweaty palms.

'Have you hired yourself a car?' she inquired. *Please don't let him say that he hasn't.* The last thing she wanted was to have to chauffeur Nicolas around.

'Of course,' he said rather drily. 'But I learned my lesson from last time and rented an SUV.'

'What do you mean, last time?'

'When I came home for Mum's funeral I hired a sports car.'

'Oh, yes, I remember,' she said. All the girls in town—and the boys—had practically salivated over the yellow sporty number parked outside the church that day. Greg had made some caustic remark. Serina had done the wise thing and ignored it.

'I presume the potholes on Rocky Creek Road are still as bad as ever,' Nicolas said.

'I'm afraid so,' she replied.

'Port's changed a lot.'

'Well, it has been a long time, Nicolas. Everything changes with time.'

'Some things not for the better,' he said rather

brusquely. 'Now, as soon as I shower and change, I'll drive out to Rocky Creek and you can show me when and where I have to go tomorrow. Then I thought I'd take you to lunch.'

'Lunch?' she practically squawked before she could think better of it. A nervous glance over at Allie and Emma showed them both nodding vigorously. To refuse would have seemed not only inhospitable, but also worthy of suspicion.

'Is there some reason why you can't do that?' he was already saying.

'Well I…I'm at work at the moment,' she hedged.

'Ah, still the demands of the family business. But surely you're the boss by now. Or did your father eventually recover from his stroke?'

Serina swallowed. 'No, no, Dad never recovered. He…um…passed away a couple of years back. Another stroke.'

'I'm so sorry, Serina,' he said softly. 'I know how much you loved him. How's your mum coping?'

Serina blinked at this surprising sensitivity from Nicolas. So different from the last time they'd spoken. At his own mother's wake, he'd been full of bitterness and anger. There'd not been one shred of understanding, or forgiveness. Maybe she was wrong about why he'd come back. Maybe he had grown mellow with age. Maybe he was well and truly over what she'd done to him all those years ago.

She hoped so. She really did.

'I think Mum was almost relieved when Dad died,' she told him. 'His quality of life was never good. He couldn't speak, you know, or walk. Therapy didn't work. The damage to his brain was too great.'

'I didn't realise that.'

Well, of course not. He'd never asked. And she'd never told him. Not that she'd had much opportunity after his stormy departure for England. There'd been no contact between them after that till the night Felicity was conceived, where their brief reunion had not exactly been filled with conversation.

Oh, why did I have to start thinking about that night?

Serina's head began to whirl. What had he just asked her? Something about her mother. Oh, yes…

'Mum's fine,' she said. 'She sold the old farm and moved into a villa in a new retirement village closer to town. She's even started working here again at the weekends, which is very good. It gives me more time to spend with Felicity.' She didn't add that all this had come about after Greg's death, when Serina hadn't felt capable of going to work for a while.

She had loved her husband. Maybe not with the type of grand passion she'd once felt for Nicolas, but it had been a very true affection.

Nevertheless, she had to confess that once she got over her initial shock and grief, Serina had experienced a strange measure of relief, the same kind of relief, no doubt, that she was sure her mother had felt after her husband had died. Her mother had become very depressed over the years, looking after her husband's needs and having little pleasure in her own life. Serina's life with Greg hadn't been as bad as that. But there was no denying her marriage had not been entirely happy. There'd been too much guilt in Serina's heart. And one very big secret, which sometimes weighed heavily on her conscience.

Now that she was widow, Serina had imagined that that secret was safe.

Till this moment…

What would Nicolas think, she suddenly worried, when he watched Felicity play the piano? And he would tomorrow night, when she performed in the talent quest. Thankfully, Felicity still looked nothing like her real father. But she had developed certain physical manner-isms when she played. Mannerisms that were horribly familiar. The flamboyant way she attacked the keys; the flourish with which she lifted her hands once she'd finished a piece; the way she tossed her hair…

It was a worry, all right.

Just when she was beginning to feel slightly more relaxed over Nicolas's motives in coming home.

'Could your mum pop in to work now, do you think?' Nicolas asked. 'Give you some time off?'

'Oh…er…no, she can't. She had to take Mrs Johnson down to Newcastle. To the John Hunter Hospital to see a heart specialist.'

'Mrs Johnson's not well?'

'Generally speaking she's very well. But she's an old lady, Nicolas. When she had a bit of a turn a few weeks back, Mum decided she should have a few tests. After what happened to Dad, she's become a strong believer in prevention being better than cure. But she won't be back till late today.'

'I see. So you're stuck at work for the rest of the day.'

'No, no, I can get away for a while,' she said when Allie and Emma started making exasperated noises. 'I have very good help here in the office. And business is rather slow at this time of the year. Not much building going on this close to Christmas.'

'That's great. I'll see you in about an hour then.'

'Fine. You know where to go?'

'I presume the lumber yard's in the same place it's always been. On the left, just past the garage at the far end of the main street.'

'Yes, that's right.' Serina could not help a wry smile pulling at her mouth. In the ten years since Nicolas's last visit to Rocky Creek, the town—plus her family's business—had changed almost as much as Port had. She would rather enjoy seeing the shock in Nicolas's eyes when he saw the changes for himself.

'You've changed, too,' she murmured not quite so happily as she inspected herself in the powder room mirror a few minutes later.

On the surface she was still an attractive woman. She hadn't put on any weight over the years. And her hair hadn't yet started turning grey. But her skin no longer held the bloom of youth. She had some lines at the corners of her eyes. And now that she looked closely, there was definitely some slackness around her jaw line.

Serina put her palms on her cheeks and her thumbs on her neck and pulled upwards, tightening her skin. That was what successful New York women did when their faces began to sag. They had facelifts and injections.

Serina dropped her hands away from her face with an exasperated sigh. She was being silly. And vain. All because of Nicolas.

Normally, she didn't wear much makeup to work, just a touch of mascara and lipstick. This morning, however, she'd surrendered to temptation and used a little foundation and some eyeliner. She'd also worn a new outfit, bought at one of the boutiques in Port Macquarie the previous weekend, one of two outfits purchased with Nicolas's visit in mind.

Feminine pride had demanded she look her best and not like some country bumpkin.

Serina's hand trembled as she went to retouch her lipstick, her fingers freezing when her eyes met her own in the mirror.

They were bright. Too bright.

'Oh, Serina, Serina, be careful,' she whispered.

She'd claimed to Nicolas that time changed everything. But nothing had changed for her where he was concerned. She still wanted him. She would always want him.

But she would not let him know that. She could not let him know that. For if she did, who knew what might happen…

CHAPTER FIVE

NICOLAS'S mind wasn't on his surroundings as he set out for the half-hour drive to Rocky Creek. It wasn't as though he didn't know the way. There was only the one road which connected Port Macquarie to Wauchope: the Oxley Highway. His thoughts were on Serina's attitude on the phone.

She hadn't seemed too upset by his return, though clearly she hadn't wanted to be personally involved with it. She'd sounded rather reluctant to go to lunch with him today. But she couldn't really say no, not without being rude.

Her daughter would not have been pleased with her mother if she'd been less than hospitable, something Nicolas was well aware of when he'd rung.

Nicolas smiled when he thought of the emails he'd exchanged with Felicity. What a delightful and intelligent child she was. But very strong-willed, if he was any judge. A handful for a widowed mother. What Felicity wanted, Felicity would contrive to get.

Nicolas knew first-hand about wilful children: he'd been one.

His own mother, who'd been a widow of sorts, had given up with him entirely by the time he was thirteen. After which he'd run his own race, on the whole, very successfully.

Only with Serina had he failed. Twice he'd let her get away. The first time through fate. Her father's stroke had made it very difficult for her to leave Australia with him. He had eventually understood that, as he'd understood how loneliness might have forced her into the arms of someone else. He hadn't exactly lived a celibate life over the years himself.

The second time he'd let her get away, Nicolas had blamed himself entirely. He should have gone after her, regardless of what she'd said in that note. He should have rocketed back to Rocky Creek, made a scene and demanded she marry him instead. He should have left no stone unturned in trying to win back the woman he loved.

Because, of course, he'd still loved her back then.

It seemed totally illogical that he still wanted her today.

But he did, heaven help him.

'And you're not going to let her get away this time, Nick, my boy,' he muttered determinedly.

Nicolas suspected, however, that Serina wasn't about to fall into his arms the way she had that night in Sydney. Thirteen years had gone by since then, thirteen long years, and ten since they'd last met. Though one could hardly count that occasion, with her husband hovering in the background.

But there was no husband now. No one to plague Nicolas's conscience if he was reduced to using sex to win her, which he might have to.

The Serina he'd spoken to just now was a lot more self-assured than the teenage Serina who'd willingly gone along with his plans.

But she was still his Serina. She might not think that there was anything left between them but she was wrong. The girl who'd never said no to him—at least where sex was concerned—was about to be awakened once more.

Nicolas's flesh stirred as he recalled the things they'd done together. In the beginning, their lovemaking had been extremely basic. But with time and practice they'd gradually known no bounds. Sometimes when he'd come home from Sydney for the weekend and Serina's parents had been out playing golf, they'd spent the whole afternoon making love all over her place…though never in her parents' room.

Nowhere else, however, was deemed sacrosanct from their increasingly erotic activities: the guest bedroom where there was a brass bed; the large squashy sofa; the rug in front of the fireplace; the coffee table…

And she'd been with him all the way.

It had been amazing—and highly addictive.

Which was why she'd come to him that night less than a month before her marriage. Because she hadn't been able to forget how it had been between them. Because she'd missed the way he'd been able to make her lose herself whilst making love.

She'd called it self-destructive, what they'd shared.

Maybe it had been. Because he'd never been totally happy with any other woman. Now that he thought about it, Nicolas suspected Serina hadn't been happy with her husband, either. The day of his mother's funeral, Serina's tension had been more than fear that she might expose what she'd done to her husband because that old chemistry had been there simmering between them.

That was what he wanted to believe, anyway. And until he had proof otherwise, Nicolas was going to believe it.

Damn it all, he had an erection now. He really had to stop thinking about sex with Serina, or things might become embarrassing.

The temperature outside was hovering around thirty degrees already. He'd boarded the plane in chilly London wearing a suit, cashmere topcoat and scarf. In Sydney, however, he'd had to start taking things off, after having to board the connecting domestic flight by exiting the air-conditioned terminal and walking across a short space of much warmer tarmac. It had been even hotter by the time he'd landed at Port Macquarie, with the clear blue sky promising an even higher temperature later in the day. Which was why he'd changed into light trousers and an open-necked shirt rolled up to the elbows.

When he'd first climbed into the rented four-wheel drive for the trip to Rocky Creek, Nicolas had felt both refreshed and relatively relaxed.

Not so anymore.

Grimacing at his discomfort, he bent forward to turn up the air-conditioning to the max. Some very cold air blasted forth and it helped clear his mind from thoughts of Serina so he could concentrate on where he was going.

Wauchope loomed up ahead, the town closest to Rocky Creek, where Nicolas had attended high school and where most of the people in Rocky Creek came to shop. He glanced around left and right, not noticing the kind of major changes he'd seen in Port. The railway crossing was still the same, as was the main street. It wasn't till he was heading out of town along the highway that he could see that the houses went farther out than they had before. There was also a big new shopping centre opposite the Timber Town tourist park.

Wauchope's prosperity had once relied solely on the timber from the surrounding forests. The trees would be cut down and the logs brought out of the hills by bullock trains, then floated down the Hastings River to Port Macquarie. Not so anymore. But you could still see demonstrations of the old ways at Timber Town, as well as buy all kinds of wood products.

Nicolas was thinking about the wooden bowl he'd once bought his mother for her birthday when he drove right past the turn off to Rocky Creek. Swearing, he pulled over to the side of the road, having to wait for several cars to go by before he could execute a U-turn. Finally, he was back at the T-intersection and heading for home.

No, not home, he amended in his mind. Rocky Creek had never been his home.

Nicolas had been born and bred in Sydney, the offspring of a brief affair between his forty-year-old mother—who'd been working as wardrobe mistress for the Sydney Opera Company at that time—and a visiting Swedish conductor who'd had a wife and family back home and a roving eye whenever he was on tour.

The conductor's eyes had landed on Madeline Dupre, who'd still been an attractive-looking woman at forty. Her lack of success so far in relationships, however, had left her somewhat embittered about the male sex, giving her a brusque manner that men had found off-putting. She'd been rather taken aback, but secretly elated, by the conductor's interest in her and had happily comforted him in bed during his stay in Sydney, deliberately deceiving him about being on the pill. She'd waved him off a few weeks later at the airport, well satisfied with her rather impulsive but successful plan to have a child by a man who would be conveniently absent from her life, but who was both handsome and intelligent. She hadn't realised at the time that raising a child by herself—especially one like Nicolas—would be so difficult.

After quitting her job during her pregnancy, she'd set about earning her living as a dressmaker. That way she could be home to look after her son. She'd already had the foresight five years earlier to get into the property market, purchasing a small though rather run-down terraced house in the inner-city suburb of Surry Hills. The deposit had taken her life savings and there was a twenty-five-year mortgage, but it had given her a sense of security. She'd patted herself on the back now that she was having a baby.

Sydney, however, was a harsh city for a woman alone. Madeline's parents had passed away—longevity did not run in her family—and her only brother had moved to western Australia to find work and had not exactly been a good communicator. All her friends had drifted away when she stopped being part of their working and social life, leaving her increasingly lonely. All she'd had in the world was her son, who'd proved to be more than she'd bargained for.

When Nicolas had been eleven—and becoming more difficult to control with each passing day—she'd made a dress for a regular client's sister who was visiting from a small town on the north coast called Rocky Creek.

'If there was a dressmaker of your skills in my home town,' the woman had gushed, 'she'd never be out of work.'

Madeline had often thought about living in the country, but just hadn't found the courage to make such a big change. She herself had been born in Sydney and had known nothing else but city life. But the problems she was encountering with Nicolas—he was getting in with a gang of boys who roamed the streets at night—forced her to look seriously at getting him away from the bad influences in the less than salubrious suburb where they lived.

Assured that she'd be able to buy a house in Rocky Creek for half of what her Surry Hills place was worth, Madeline made the massive decision to up stakes and move from Sydney to the country.

Nicolas had been furious with her. He was a city boy through and through. He didn't want to live out in the sticks. He didn't want to go to a school that had less than sixty children. He complained—and played up—at considerable length.

Till Mrs Johnson—and the piano—came into his life.

Despite being known as Mrs Johnson, the piano teacher was actually a childless spinster who lived in the house next door to the small cottage in Rocky Creek that his mother had bought. She gave private piano lessons for a living and had reputedly once been a not so very famous concert pianist. As fate would have it, her music room was just over the fence from Nicolas's bedroom. He could not help hearing the music.

For ages, Nicolas had not understood why he liked it so much. Up till then his musical taste had stopped at rock and heavy metal. One day— he'd just turned twelve—he hadn't been able to resist the pull of the music any longer, so he'd asked his mother if he could have piano lessons.

Despite not having any spare money for music lessons—or a piano—a delighted Madeline Dupre had quickly come to an agreement with

Mrs Johnson, who would teach Nicolas for nothing if Madeline made her a dress whenever she needed one. As for a piano, Mrs Johnson had also agreed that Nicolas could practise on hers whenever it was free. Once she'd realised she had a prodigy on her hands, the ecstatic teacher had even gave him a front door key so that he could let himself in when she was out playing bridge.

Soon Nicolas was practising every chance he got. He'd rarely done any of his homework but he'd excelled at the piano. At the age of fifteen he'd passed seventh grade with honours. By seventeen he'd received his Licentiate Diploma of Music, the highest musical exam one could take in Australia. During his last year in high school he'd sat for—and won—a scholarship to the Sydney Conservatorium of Music.

Mrs Johnson had been extremely proud of him, as had been his mother. But no one else in Rocky Creek had cared all that much. Why? Because he was an outsider. He'd always been an outsider, not a true local. At school, he'd never joined in, or played sports, made friends, had a girlfriend. All he'd cared about was playing the piano.

Serina was the only girl he'd ever bothered to speak to.

Serina again…

Nicolas scooped in a deep breath, then let it out very slowly. It was a toss-up, he decided, who had seduced whom that first night. Serina had confessed to him once that she'd had a wild crush on him since their paths had crossed when he was twelve and she was only nine. She'd told him she used to organise her own music lessons so that they came after his. She would arrive early and sit in Mrs Johnson's lounge room and listen to him play. He'd hardly noticed her back then. Gradually, however, they had exchanged a few words and in the end he'd quite looked forward to their conversations. Once, Mrs Johnson had taught them a duet, which they'd performed at the Rocky Creek annual fete to much applause.

Though not as good as he was, Serina had been an accomplished pianist. It did not surprise him that her daughter was taking piano lessons now. What did surprise him was that Mrs Johnson was her teacher. She'd have to be about a hundred years old by now.

Well, at least over eighty. She must have been

about sixty twenty-five years ago. Or so Nicolas had thought at the time. Still, when you're young, anyone over forty seems old.

Now he was almost forty himself. The years were flying by. And so was this rotten damned road.

Hitting a pothole reminded him to slow down and to put his mind on his driving. He slowed down even further to negotiate a series of hairpin bends, which he knew would take him down into the valley and Rocky Creek.

It had always been a pretty little town, he'd give it that, and quite conveniently located, being only ten minutes from the train line at Wauchope and half an hour from Port Macquarie, with its beaches and airport. But it was too small for his liking. Too small in size and in thinking. Everyone knew everything about everyone in Rocky Creek. He hated that. He loved the privacy—even the anonymity—that cities like London and New York could provide. Not to mention the wide range of entertainment. He could not imagine ever living anywhere else.

So what are you doing here, Nicolas? came the sudden thought.

Serina's not still in love with you and she's

never going to come with you. Not ever. You
know that. She is a local and so is her daughter.
You're wasting your time.

It was a bitter pill to swallow, the truth. But
swallow it, Nicolas did. He also faced another
truth, the real reason why he'd come, why he'd
rented that luxury apartment. Why he'd con-
trived to be alone with her today.

Because he just had to be with Serina one more
time.

Nicolas glanced at his scarred and thumbless
left hand and remembered how it had been for
him, accepting that he would never play the
piano again. For a while he'd been in total
despair. But in the end he'd had to accept it,
because he couldn't change that. He couldn't
grow another thumb.

But he could be with Serina again. Maybe only
for a few hours, but it was possible. And whilst
it was possible, nothing short of death was going
to stop him from achieving that end.

The road swung round one last bend before
straightening and heading down a more gentle
incline. The thick bush on either side thinned out
a little and Nicolas caught a glimpse of house
after house between the tall trees.

Nicolas's eyebrows arched. They certainly hadn't been there ten years ago. His surprise increased as he drove slowly over the wooden bridge that forded the creek and led straight into the main street of Rocky Creek. Now his eyes widened as he noted the massive number of shop fronts. There was a tea house he'd never seen before, an antique shop and a very swish-looking beauty salon. There was another new café, with alfresco tables and chairs on the foot path. Even the old general store—which had been built in 1880—had been modernised with a separate fruit-and-vegetable shop next door to it.

The butcher was basically the same, as was the bakery.

But everything looked brighter and more prosperous.

The old garage at the end of the main street had received a facelift as well. But none of those things prepared him for the changes to Ted Brown's Lumber Yard.

Firstly, it wasn't called that anymore. The new sign facing the road shouted Brown's Landscaping and Building Supplies in bold red letters. The old shed, which had once housed a ramshackle office, had been replaced by a smart cream brick building. To the right of this building sat huge piles of sand, gravel, coloured stones and mulches of various kinds. To the left was a large array of brick, tiles and paving samples to choose from. In front was a tarred car park, the parking spaces neatly marked out with lines, a far cry from what had once been a dirt paddock with a rutted driveway that turned to mud in the wet weather. Visible over the roof of the cream building stood the timber supply section, which had to be double the height and size that it used to be.

Nicolas smiled a wry smile as he angled his vehicle into one of the parking spaces. Serina could have warned him. But he supposed seeing the changes for himself was worth a thousand words.

A sudden and not very nice thought popped into his head.

Maybe Rocky Creek wasn't the only thing that had made massive physical changes during the past ten years. Maybe the Serina he remembered had changed, too. Maybe she'd put on weight. Maybe she'd cut her lovely hair short and started wearing polyester tracksuits.

'Surely not,' he muttered as he switched off the

engine and extracted the key. It wasn't in her nature to let herself go. She was a perfectionist, like him. He only had to see what she'd done with the family business to know that she'd become a right little powerhouse in her own way. A woman like that would still look after her appearance.

Feeling relieved, Nicolas pushed open the driver's door, only to be met by a great whoosh of warm air.

It's hot, he thought as he climbed down from behind the wheel. Swelteringly, blisteringly hot.

Admittedly, his blood was thick because he'd been living in the northern winter. But still…how had he stood it here every summer? None of the houses or shops in Rocky Creek had had air-conditioning back then.

Nicolas shook his head and moved quickly over to the cream brick building, grateful to see two cooling units sitting by the side wall.

The girl behind the rather high and very long reception desk looked up as he entered the chilled space, her plump, plain face lighting up into a welcoming smile.

'You must be Mr Dupre,' she said chirpily.

'I am,' he agreed.

'I'm Allie. He's here, Serina,' she called out over her shoulder into the open-plan office.

Nicolas stepped closer to the chest-high counter and followed the direction of Allie's eyes.

And there she was.

His Serina, sitting behind a wide, wooden, sun-drenched desk.

His heart virtually stopped when she stood up and made her way across the room. She hadn't lost her gorgeous figure, he noted as his gaze raked her body from head to toe. She was just the same as she'd looked at his mother's funeral: lush and beautiful.

This time, however, she wasn't wearing black. Far from it. Her dress was extremely bright, emerald-green with large multicoloured flowers printed around the hem of the gathered skirt. The top was sleeveless and square-necked, a wide white belt cinching in her waist, highlighting her hourglass shape. As she walked, her hair, which was slightly shorter at shoulder length, swung like a sleek dark curtain around her slender shoulders.

The only thing that had really changed was her face. It was the face of a woman now, a woman who was clearly determined not to be bowled over by an old flame hitting town. Her eyes were decidedly cool as she approached, and there was a hint of annoyance in the firm set of her lips.

'You got here more quickly than I thought you would,' she said.

'I was anxious to see my home town again. Which, I might add, is looking wonderful. As are you,' he added, and looked hard at her mouth, that same mouth that had known every inch of his body.

Her lips pressed even more firmly together. 'You're looking very well yourself,' came her somewhat stiff reply. 'Look, I'll just get my handbag and we'll go straight over to the school, where you can meet everyone and find out where and when you have to go tomorrow.'

'Fine,' he replied, not sure what to make of her impersonal manner. 'And then we'll drive to Port for a long lunch by the water,' he added whilst he had her where he wanted her—in public. 'We can catch up on old times. That'll be all right, won't it, girls?' he said, smiling at Allie then at the other girl he'd spotted sitting at a desk not far from Serina's. 'You can cope without the boss for the rest of today, can't you?'

'Absolutely,' they chorused, beaming back at him.

'Great,' he said, and totally ignored Serina's scowl.

'Your handbag?' he prodded with a smooth smile when she just stood there, glowering at him. Sucking in sharply, she spun on her heels and stalked back to her desk.

'I'm Emma, by the way,' the other girl piped up during the time it took Serina to collect her bag.

She was the more attractive of the two, though Nicolas could have guaranteed that she was not a natural blonde. Her short spiked hair had decidedly brassy ends with dark roots.

'Lovely to meet you, Emma. And you must call me Nicolas,' he said to both of them. 'So will you two girls be at the talent quest tomorrow afternoon?'

'Are you kidding?' Emma answered. 'We wouldn't miss it for the world. Everyone in town's going, and quite a lot of people from the surrounding areas. Felicity's done a great job at promotion. She printed out hundreds of fliers on her computer and she and her friends delivered them to every post-box for miles.'

'Yes, and it cost me a small fortune in paper,' Serina grumbled on rejoining him. 'Come on, let's go.'

'See you tomorrow night, Nicolas,' Emma called after them.

'Looking forward to it,' he called back…

CHAPTER SIX

SERINA gritted her teeth as both of them stepped outside, steeling herself for a very difficult day.

'I'd forgotten how hot it can get here in the summer,' Nicolas said. 'I should have put shorts on.'

His comment drew her gaze, not just to his trousers—which were beige and elegantly cut—but his overall appearance. He'd aged very little during the last ten years. There was no extra flab to spoil his tall lean body and only a few extra lines around his eyes and mouth. No one would believe he was almost forty. He cut the same dashing figure whom she'd faced at his mother's funeral, and who'd once wowed the audiences at his concerts. He still wore his blond wavy hair down to his collar, she noted irritably, still had ridiculously long eyelashes and the bluest of blue eyes—eyes that had always set her heartbeat racing even when she was a young girl.

Her heart was racing now. It had started the moment he'd walked into the office.

Her automatic response to him annoyed the hell out of her. One would have thought that the years would have brought her more control— and a lot more common sense. All she could hope for was that her feelings weren't written all over her face.

'No need really,' she replied crisply. 'I presume your hire car has air-conditioning?' She nodded towards the dark grey SUV parked opposite them.

'Of course.'

'Then let's go get in,' she suggested, her voice cool and confident but her insides anything but.

It wasn't till they were inside the vehicle, with the engine and air-conditioning on, that she dared glance across in his direction once more. Even so she didn't look at his face. She found her decidedly uptight gaze landing on his hands as he placed them on the steering wheel.

'Oh, Nicolas!' she exclaimed before she could stop herself.

'What?' His head jerked round, his blue eyes alarmed.

'Your...your hand.'

'Ah,' he said knowingly, and lifted his left

hand from the wheel, turning it this way and that as though it was a long time since he'd looked at it himself.

There was no thumb, not even a small stump, the digit having been amputated at the second knuckle. But that wasn't all. The back of his hand was heavily scarred, the skin puckered up in places. His right hand had a few scars as well, she noted, but nothing like his left.

'Lovely, isn't it?' he said drily, and placed it back down on the wheel, his remaining knuckles showing white when his fingers curved tightly around the rim. 'Unfortunately, there are no compositions suitable for thumbless concert pianists. And to think I used to be able to span ten keys. But not to worry. It probably worked out for the best. The life of a concert pianist is very limited and limiting. I've done well enough out of my change of career.'

'Yes, I know,' Serina said, quickly pulling herself together and resolving not to go all mushy over him just because of his hand. 'I saw you being interviewed on television a couple of years ago,' she went on matter-of-factly. 'You looked very successful in your New York apartment and very prosperous.'

He gave a small laugh. 'That's the pot calling the kettle black. Just look at what you've done. Turned your dad's rather ramshackle lumber yard into a thriving business. I can see where your daughter gets her entrepreneurial skills from.'

Serina didn't know what to say to that. It took all her willpower not to look guilty.

The sound of her mobile phone ringing saved her from further embarrassment. Serina fished it out of her handbag and flipped it open.

'Yes?' she answered.

'Has he rung yet?' her daughter demanded to know in impatient tones. Too late, Serina remembered that Felicity had asked her to ring her as soon as she'd heard from Nicolas. Felicity had begged for her own personal mobile phone for her tenth birthday. And, being somewhat spoiled by Greg, she had got what she wanted.

'Yes, Felicity,' Serina said with a sigh. 'He's rung and he's here in Rocky Creek and we're on our way to the school right now. Okay? See you shortly.' And she hung up.

Nicolas smiled over at her as he fired the engine. 'That daughter of yours is quite a handful, isn't she?'

'How did you guess?' she replied frustratedly, and he laughed.

'So,' he said as he drove out of the car park and turned left. 'Is the school in the same place?'

'Yes.'

'What? No more surprises?'

'Maybe a few.'

'Perhaps you should elaborate whilst I drive. Save me from having egg all over my face. Though I suspect that's what you had in mind when you didn't warn me over the phone how much Rocky Creek had gone ahead.'

'Huh! I didn't see any egg over your face back at the office. You had those girls eating out of your hand and you know it.'

He shot her a smile that curled both her toes and her heart. 'I have learned the art of charming the ladies over the years.'

Serina was grateful that he'd reminded her in time what kind of life he'd been leading since leaving Rocky Creek. Not pining for her, that was for sure. Not even before their final but brief encounter thirteen years ago.

According to the many tabloid articles Felicity had uncovered about him on the Internet, he'd wined and dined some of the most beautiful women in show business. No doubt he'd slept with most of them as well. The Nicolas she knew would not have been living the life of a monk. Not likely!

'I am relieved,' she said in chilly tones. 'Just make sure you don't use up all that much-learned charm before tomorrow. I would hate you to turn into one of those judges who think they have to be cruel to be kind.'

Although Nicolas was slightly taken aback by her sarcasm, he was also heartened, as he had been by her obvious annoyance back at her office. She was trying very hard to be cool but her frosty politeness didn't fool him for a minute. He could feel the sexual tension that she was desperately trying to hide. If he hadn't had at that moment turned in to the street where the school was, he would have pulled over to the side of the road and kissed her senseless.

'Now, as you can see,' she went on as he drove along the tree-lined road, 'the old school is still there. But when our enrolment trebled a few years back, the government finally built us a new school next to it that incorporates an office, several classrooms and a great big school hall, which has a decent stage and room for five hundred seats. That's where we're holding the talent quest.'

'With air-conditioning?' he inquired.

'Of course,' she said haughtily. 'Gus paid for that.'

'Gus?' Nicolas echoed. 'Surely you don't mean old wino Gus.' Old Gus had been a harmless drunk who'd slept in the sports shed and whom the kids had looked after with food, blankets and clothes.

'Yep. Turned out he was a secret millionaire. When he died back in 2005, he left all his money to the Rocky Creek Parents' and Citizens' Association. We don't touch the capital, which is wisely invested. But, with the interest so far, we've air-conditioned the school, kitted out a great computer room, cleared some of the bush behind and built a soccer field and two netball courts. Now we're saving up to put in a swimming pool.'

'We? Does that mean you're on the committee of the P and C?'

'Of course I am,' she told him. 'I'm the treasurer.'

Nicolas tried not to be dismayed by her involvement with the community, but failed. The more she told him, the more he realised that nothing was going to get Serina away from Rocky Creek. She was entrenched here.

But then you knew that, didn't you, Nick, my boy?

It was why she'd rejected you, not once, but twice. Because she preferred life here to the life you craved. Because she loved her family—and Rocky Creek—more than you.

Maybe if she'd been a childless widow, he might have stood a chance. But she wasn't. She was a mother. Mother love, Nicolas knew from experience, was much stronger than anything he could ever evoke in her.

But alongside his dismay lay the same kind of determination with which Nicolas had always faced life and life's challenges. He might not have any future with Serina. But no way was he going to leave Australia without holding her in his arms once more, without experiencing one more time their unique brand of chemistry— and it was unique. Nicolas had never felt anything like it. They'd once shared a stunning degree of physical intimacy and sexual pleasure that could never be forgotten. He hadn't forgotten it and he was damned sure Serina hadn't. She was just pretending that she had.

But he would remind her during their lunch together.

First, however, he had to get this visit to the school over and done with.

Nicolas pulled the SUV into the curb outside the school's front gate, and stared up at the ancient sign, which said it had been established in 1870. The old school was made of wood, a rectangular building with a highpitched roof and a north-facing verandah that had pegs on the wall where the children could hang their hats and school bags. There'd only been four class-rooms when he'd gone to school there, with composite classes the order of the day.

Admittedly, he'd only attended Rocky Creek primary for one year, but he hadn't been happy there. He'd still been sulking because of their move from Sydney and he hadn't yet discovered the joys of the piano. He recalled going on a hunger strike at one stage, giving all his food to a very grateful Gus. When no one appeared to care whether he starved or not, he started eating again.

Nicolas was not one to bash his head against a brick wall for long. Once reality sank into his head, he accepted it and moved on. Which was probably why he hadn't pursued Serina those two times she'd rejected him. He'd actually believed her when she'd said she didn't want him. Believed there was no point in going after her. Pride hadn't been the only issue.

But there was wanting and wanting. Her love for him had obviously been found wanting. But what of her lust?

The speed with which she bolted out of the SUV once he'd stopped suggested she hadn't enjoyed being alone with him in a confined space.

'You might as well leave your bag behind,' he suggested as he climbed out from behind the wheel and slammed the door. 'We're going to lunch together shortly, remember?'

Her body language showed extreme irritation with him. She clutched the bag even more tightly in her right hand and threw him what could only be described as a wintry look. 'I don't recall agreeing to do any such thing.'

The possibility of her not even going to lunch with him did not sit well with Nicolas. 'It will look odd, if you don't. Emma and Allie won't be pleased. Neither will Felicity. What are you afraid of, Serina? That I'll throw you across the restaurant table and have my wicked way with you right in front of everyone?'

'Don't be ridiculous,' she snapped. 'I'm well aware that the days of my being your sexual cup of tea are long gone. This way,' she said coldly, and marched off through the front gate and along a path that led past the old school and across to an L-shaped cream brick building sitting where the playground had once been.

An increasingly frustrated Nicolas stalked after her, grudgingly noting that the surrounds of the new Rocky Creek primary school were a credit to the P & C. Covered walkways ran everywhere, protecting the children from rain as well as the hot summer sun. The gardens and lawns were both immaculate and alive, obviously having an excellent watering system.

'Very nice landscaping,' he remarked.

'Gus's money also pays for a gardener,' she said.

'Good old Gus.'

'There's no need to be sarcastic!'

'I wasn't,' Nicolas denied, although he recognised his mood had shifted to a darker place, that place where he was propelled when things didn't go his way, or when he looked like he was failing at something.

Serina stopped walking and whirled to face him, her dark eyes stormy. 'Look, I know what you think of Rocky Creek. It's written all over your supercilious face. No matter how much the town's progressed, you still think of it as a backwater with nothing here to interest you. Which is absolutely true. We don't have an opera house or theatres galore, or mansions full of the rich and famous who hold dinner parties every day of the week. We don't have expensive art galleries, museums or designer boutiques. We certainly don't have super highways where you can drive at two hundred kilometres an hour in your two-hundred-thousand-dollar sports cars. What we do have, however, is people who care about each other. People who are loving and loyal, people who look after each other when times are tough and who are prepared to make sacrifices. Who don't always think of their own selfish selves!'

Nicolas stood there, stunned by the savagery of Serina's tirade.

She seemed a little stunned herself. 'I'm sorry,' she said at last, if a little grudgingly. 'I guess that was rude of me. The thing is, Nicolas, I just don't understand why you agreed to come all this way for a silly little talent quest. Other than your brief visit when your mum died, you haven't darkened the doorstep of Rocky Creek for over twenty years!'

He looked deep into her eyes and ached to tell her the truth.

I came because I still want you, Serina. Because I wanted to make love to you again. I came because I just couldn't stay away, not once I knew you weren't married anymore.

But it wasn't the right time, or the right place. It might never be the right time, or the right place, he realised grimly. Not if she felt this viciously about him.

'I came,' he said instead, quite truthfully as well, 'because of your daughter's very touching letter.'

And, right on cue, Felicity came flying down the path towards them.

Nicolas knew she was Felicity because it was like seeing Serina at that age, so great was the resemblance.

'You're here!' Felicity squealed as only a twelve-year-old girl can squeal. She didn't stop there, either, literally throwing herself against him so hard that he lurched backwards a step.

'Oh, thank you, thank you, thank you!' she blurted, hugging him tightly around the waist before abruptly disengaging herself and throwing him a sheepish look from under her long lashes. 'Sorry. I get a bit carried away sometimes. Don't I, Mum…?'

CHAPTER SEVEN

SERINA would have loved to turn tail and run at that point. It had already been getting to be too much for her, seeing Nicolas again. That had been why she'd let fly at him just now, because she'd needed some outlet for the tension building inside her.

Serina had expected today to be difficult. And she'd been right. But nothing had prepared her for what she'd just witnessed.

Seeing her daughter hug her biological father had produced a mixture of emotions that threatened to overwhelm her. Perversely, she almost felt jealous of Felicity. How she would love to hug Nicolas with such unashamed delight! At the same time a great wave of guilt twisted at her insides. She should never have passed Felicity off as Greg's daughter. Never! She should have told the truth from the start. Instead, she'd locked herself into a secret that was going to crucify her now till her dying days.

Because she'd seen the flash of joy in Nicolas's face when his daughter had wrapped her arms tightly around him, seen the gently indulgent way he'd smiled down at her. He was still smiling at her.

The unexpected realisation that Nicolas might have been a good father to Felicity was shattering.

But it was too late now. It had been too late from the moment she'd walked down that church aisle with Greg all those years ago. Her secret had to continue. Because in Felicity's mind, Greg Harmon was her father, not Nicolas. She'd loved Greg, and she loved Greg's parents—they were her adored Nanna and Pop. No, the secret had to be kept.

She had to pull herself together and not act like some guilt-ridden, broken-hearted fool, even if what she wanted to do was fall in a crumpled heap on this path and cry.

Amazing what a mother could endure when faced with the possibility of her child's unhappiness. So Serina found a smile from somewhere and a voice that sounded close to normal.

'There's nothing wrong with being enthusiastic, Felicity,' she said. 'But it might be wise not to be too familiar with Mr Dupre. Otherwise people might say there's favouritism if you come first in the talent quest tomorrow night.'

Too late Serina wished she hadn't brought up that subject.

'I've already thought of that,' Felicity returned. 'So I've decided not to enter.'

'I think that's a wise decision,' Serina said, hiding her relief behind a genuinely warm smile.

'But I was looking forward to hearing you play,' Nicolas protested.

'Oh, you'll still hear me play,' Felicity informed him quite happily. 'I'm giving a special performance at the end of the talent quest. I don't want to tell you too much except that it's a tribute to a certain concert pianist who sadly can't play anymore.'

Serina smothered a groan of despair. Not only was Felicity going to play for him, but she was also sure to choose one of Nicolas's favourites, maybe even the Chopin Polonaise both of them had heard him play on the Internet. If today was proving difficult, tomorrow loomed as a nightmare!

'Come on, Nicolas,' Felicity said. 'It's time for you to meet everyone else.'

'Felicity!' Serina protested. 'You shouldn't be using Mr Dupre's first name.'

'It's perfectly all right, Serina,' Nicolas remarked.

'No, it's not,' Serina protested. 'It is my job to teach my daughter respect for her elders.'

'In that case she can call Mrs Johnson, Mrs Johnson,' Nicolas shot back, his face irritated. 'I'm not yet forty and don't consider myself an elder just yet. So if you don't mind, I'd prefer to be called Nicolas. Lead on, Felicity, my dear,' he concluded, and actually took his daughter's hand.

Felicity beamed with smug satisfaction whilst Serina felt like strangling her. And Nicolas. Perhaps it was a survival mechanism, but suddenly her mood changed from one of distress to a simmering fury. Whereas before she hadn't been looking forward to having lunch with him, now she was. It would give her the opportunity to say all the things she'd bottled up about him over the years. Her brief tirade of a minute ago was just the tip of the iceberg. There were lots of questions she'd always wanted answered. Specifically why, if he'd loved her so much, he hadn't come back for her from England all those years ago? Why at least he hadn't written!

But the critical question was why hadn't he pursued her after their last extremely passionate encounter. Any man as in love as he'd expressed himself to be that night should have ignored her letter and come after her anyway.

No wonder she'd married Greg!

Clenching her teeth, she trudged up the path after Felicity—and her daughter's unsuspecting father—and into the school hall, where she pasted a plastic smile on her face and watched with growing resentment whilst Nicolas charmed the socks off everyone there.

There were lots of people in the hall that morning. All the teachers, all of the mothers who didn't work, a few husbands who'd taken time off to help put all the plastic chairs in rows and quite a number of children. Serina might have marvelled at Nicolas's social skills if she hadn't already witnessed him in action back at the office. He hadn't always been Mister Warmth and Charm. But there was no doubt he'd learned how to deal with people over the years. He was smooth, very smooth.

He'd been smooth during that television interview a couple of years back, she recalled. But that wasn't the same as seeing him in action in the flesh. In no time he had everyone eating out of his hands. Felicity, especially.

'Isn't he awesome, Mum?' she gushed at one stage when Nicolas was off to one side, chatting with the principal. 'And so good-looking. Do you think he has a girlfriend back in New York?'

'I would imagine so,' Serina said, surprised that this thought hadn't entered her mind earlier. Surprised, too, at the hurt it brought.

'Probably that Japanese violinist,' Felicity went on, blissfully unaware of her mother's agitation. 'She's very pretty. I'll ask him.'

'Don't you dare!' Serina snapped. 'That would be very rude.'

'Oh. Do you think so? Well you could ask him, Mum. Later, when you're at lunch together.'

Serina rolled her eyes. 'Who told you I was going to lunch with him?'

'Nicolas did. Just now.'

'I see,' she said with an exasperated sigh. 'I suppose I might be able to find out. But why on earth do you want to know?'

Felicity's expression turned a little sly. 'Well, I was thinking that if he didn't have a girlfriend, then you and he might...you know...get together again. I mean…you were once boy-friend and girlfriend.'

'For pity's sake, Felicity, how many times do I have to tell you that we only dated a few times!'

'That's not what Mrs Johnson said. She told me you were as thick as thieves in the old days. And Nana said you cried for weeks after he went to London to study.'

'You know, Felicity, you shouldn't listen to small-town gossip. Nicolas and I were just good friends, like I told you. We were not romantically involved. As for my crying when he went overseas, Mum's mistaken about that entirely. It was around that time that your grandpa had his stroke and I was very upset. My crying had nothing to do with Nicolas leaving Rocky Creek. You've got it all wrong, missy. So please don't try to do what those two silly girls in my office are doing and match-make me up with every eligible man who happens to cross my path. I loved your father very much and I don't wish to date, or get married again, especially not to Nicolas Dupre. Do I make myself clear?'

Felicity had the good grace to hang her head at this dressing down. Unfortunately, this allowed Serina a direct view over the top of her daughter's drooped head right into Nicolas's piercing blue eyes.

'I'm all finished here,' he said, his facial expression bland.

Hopefully, he hadn't heard that last, rather savage remark. But Serina suspected that he had.

'Mr Tarleton said I was to be here tomorrow at one-thirty,' Nicolas went on crisply. 'Is that early enough, Felicity?'

'Heaps early enough. The talent quest doesn't start till two. You'll stay for the party afterwards, won't you?'

'Of course. Now I'm off to take your mother to lunch. We're going to spend the afternoon in Port Macquarie, catching up on old times.'

Serina flashed him a sour glance before smiling at her daughter. 'I'll be home no later than four, sweetie,' she said. 'Will you be finished setting up the hall by then?'

'Oh, yes. Easily. We're almost done now. But Kirsty wants to rehearse her acts for tomorrow. I'm going to practise as well. One of the pieces I've chosen to play is really hard.'

'You're making me very curious over what you're going to play,' Nicolas said.

Felicity looked smug. 'Sorry. Can't tell. And you're not to tell him, either, Mum.'

'How can I when I don't know myself?' Serina replied somewhat starchily.

'That's good,' Felicity said with a brilliant smile. ''Bye now. See you when you get home.' And she ran off to join her friends.

'I suspect you do know what she's going to play,' Nicolas said as he clamped a firm hand around her right elbow and started steering her towards the side door. 'And you're not happy about it for some reason. The same way you're not happy about my returning to Rocky Creek.'

'I see no reason why I should be happy?' she retorted once they were outside and out of earshot of other people.

'Maybe not,' he bit out. 'But there's no reason why it should overly bother you, either. There's no husband to object to our reunion. Or any new boyfriend, from what I just overheard.'

Serina wrenched out of his hold and ground to a halt. 'Our reunion?' She glared up into his eyes. 'We are not having any kind of reunion here. If I had my way we wouldn't even be having lunch together. But you manipulated things so that I couldn't say no without being rude. As for catching up on old times…don't go thinking that's ever going to happen, Nicolas Dupre. I wouldn't let you touch me again if you were the last man on earth!'

Serina knew the second that last statement fell out of her mouth that she'd gone too far. Way too far.

A cruel smile began at the corners of his eyes. His coldly glittering blue eyes.

'I'll remind you what you just said later today. But for now, I would suggest that you shut that beautiful mouth of yours. Because whilst you might not want to date me ever again, or God forbid, marry me, I'm pretty sure you do want to go to bed with me. In fact, I'm absolutely certain of it.'

Serina's mouth gasped open. She was on the verge of hotly denying his arrogant statement—despite it being appallingly true—when she spotted a couple of the mothers standing at one of the school hall windows, staring over at them. The time to do battle was not right now, she quickly appreciated, and snapped her gaping mouth shut.

'Glad to see you've finally found some common sense,' he ground out. 'And some

honesty. Let's go.' And taking forceful posses-
sion of her elbow once more, he propelled her
along the path that led them past the old school
and back to the parked SUV…

CHAPTER EIGHT

NICOLAS knew—as one always knew deep down—that he'd just crossed a line; that line that you didn't step over if you were a gentleman.

But then he'd never been a gentleman. And he never would be one, despite having smoothed away most of his rough edges over the years. He spoke like a gentlemen these days and dressed like one. His town house in London was the home of a gentleman. His New York apartment, however, reeked of new money, the kind made by men who hadn't been born rich, but who'd made it in the world by talent and tenacity. Men who were winners, men who knew what they wanted and went after it.

What he'd just said to Serina had been provocative in the extreme, provocative and presumptuous. And risky. By speaking up so boldly, he'd ruined any chance of a romantic seduction.

But in that moment before she'd been able to hide the truth, when her body and mind had still been reeling from the shock of his words, he'd glimpsed her ongoing sexual vulnerability to him. What he'd just said had been right. She did want to go to bed with him.

Serina didn't say a single word during the short time it took to steer her back to the car. But her body language reeked of rebellion. Nicolas's own body was consumed by something else....

Serina snatched her arm away from his hold before climbing up into the SUV and banging the door shut behind her. She refused to look at him as he got in behind the wheel, refused to speak. Instead, she stuffed her handbag at her feet and crossed her arms, glaring balefully out of the passenger window.

'You'd better put your seat belt on,' Nicolas advised as he did so himself then started up the engine.

She did so huffily, still not looking his way, Rocky Creek well behind them before her simmering fury found a path to her tongue.

'I was right all along,' she blustered, her head finally turning in his direction. 'You didn't come back out of kindness, or generosity. You came back for revenge!'

Her accusation produced a startling result, Nicolas's eyes leaving the road at an inopportune time, since they were on a sharp corner at the time. The left-side wheels slid off the narrow strip of tar, spitting gravel out behind them. The back of the vehicle began to slide, Nicolas swearing as he struggled for control.

The adrenalin of fear and panic had Serina gripping her seat belt whilst visions of their careering off the road and into a steep gully—or the bone-crunching trunk of a gum tree—flashed before her mind.

'And I was right,' Nicolas snarled when he finally had them safely back on the road. 'You're going to be the death of me one day. I think I'll find a place to stop before we continue this rather amazing conversation.'

Serina didn't object. She was still shaking inside when he pulled over into a lay-by and turned off the engine.

'Now,' he said firmly as he undid his seat belt and turned towards her. 'What's all this nonsense about revenge?'

Serina stared into his beautiful blue eyes and

saw nothing dark or deceptive. Only confusion. Which confused her.

'Revenge for what?' he demanded to know.

'For...for what I did that night,' she spluttered.

'Ah,' he said, and nodded. 'You're still feeling guilty about that, are you?'

'Of course! What I did that night...it was very wrong.'

'Are we talking about what you did to me? Or what you did to your husband?'

Serina stiffened. 'Greg wasn't my husband at that stage.'

'That's semantics, Serina, and you know it. You were unfaithful to your soon-to-be husband that night. And you deceived me.'

A guilty frustration swamped her, making her head whirl and her heart twist. 'I didn't mean to do either,' she blurted out. 'I...I just couldn't help myself.' Tears of dismay and despair filled her eyes. 'It all happened by accident.'

Nicolas's expression was sceptical. 'You just happened to be at my concert. Is that what you're saying?'

'No. Yes. I mean...I came to Sydney for a couple of days shopping for my wedding and I saw you being interviewed on television. One of those morning programs. I heard you were playing at the Opera House that night and I thought…what would be the harm? I just want to see him one more time,' she choked out, as though she were talking to someone else. Confessing, perhaps, to a priest. 'But then I watched you perform and I…I knew I had to do more than just see you….' The tears spilled over then and trickled down her cheeks. 'I couldn't help it, Nicolas. I'm not a bad person. And I'm sorry, truly sorry.'

He reached over and gently wiped the tears from her face. 'I won't say that what you did didn't hurt me. It did. Terribly. But I can see that I hurt you, too, by staying away in the first place. I should have come back for you earlier.'

'Why didn't you?' she said with a tormented groan.

'Male pride, mostly. You said you didn't want me.'

A small laugh escaped her lips. 'And you believed me?'

Nicolas smiled a rather sad smile. 'Yes, Serina, I believed you. But that's water under the bridge now, isn't it? We can't go back and undo anything in the past. All we can control is the here and now. So let me redress something I told you a little while ago, about why I'm here. Yes, it was because of your daughter's letter. But not for the reason I let you think. I haven't come all this way to help Felicity raise money for your local bushfire brigade. I could have easily sent a cheque to do that. I came because your daughter told me that her father—your husband, Greg—is now dead. I came because of you, Serina. Let's not have any misunderstandings about that.'

Serina tried to work some saliva into her suddenly dry mouth. It was what she both craved and feared.

'But it's too late,' she told him.

'Too late for what?'

'For us...'

'It's never too late, Serina. Not whilst we're still alive.'

'You don't understand.'

'Are you saying that you don't want me anymore?'

She could not help the sensual shudder that rippled down her spine.

'You have to give me another chance, Serina,' he proclaimed.

'I won't leave Rocky Creek,' she insisted wildly. 'I won't, I tell you.'

'I'm not asking you to,' he said. 'Just come back to Port Macquarie for the afternoon.'

She stared at him, her eyes wide.

'I can't!' she protested huskily.

His smile was sexy. 'Of course you can. We're already going there for lunch.'

'You're not talking about lunch, though, are you?'

'No. No, Serina, I'm not.'

The image his words evoked took her breath away. 'You're wicked. You were always wicked!'

'Oh, come now, Serina, don't go all holier-than-thou on me. I never did a single thing you didn't want me to. Or beg me to.'

'I never begged!'

'Then perhaps it's high time you did. Shall I make you beg this afternoon, my love?'

Serina knew she had to fight the insidious desires that were already invading her. For if she gave in to what he wanted…

She shuddered to think of the consequences, both to her life and her future happiness. Not to mention the happiness of her child.

'How can you possibly put words like *love* and *beg* in the same sentence?' she argued fiercely. 'You have no idea what love is, Nicolas Dupre. You never really loved me. I meant no more to you than your piano. I was just an instrument to be mastered. You practised making love to me the way you used to practise your scales. Till your technique was perfect. But you never cared for me enough to make me any kind of priority. Your career always came first. When our relationship became difficult, you chose your career over me and moved on. You did the same thing when fate intervened and cut short your concert career. You moved on. Very successfully, too. Yet if you'd truly loved playing the piano, that accident would have come close to destroying you. But it didn't, did it? You rose again, like the Phoenix, and made an even greater success of your life. Which is commendable in a way. But it shows a certain ruthlessness of character, which I know I can't live with. Or love.'

Her stomach contracted a little at this last lie. Because, of course, she did love Nicolas. Always had and always would. But the other things she'd just said weren't lies. He was not the kind of man a woman could rely on to make her happy.

Serina hadn't reached the age of thirty-six without becoming a reasonable judge of character.

Nicolas was selfish and self-centred. He might not have come back for revenge, but he had come back to win. She was the one who'd got away. That was why he'd been so angry with her at his mother's funeral. Because she'd rejected him, not once but twice. A man like Nicolas didn't take rejection lightly, a fact made obvious by the expression on his face.

'So you won't give me another chance,' he said grimly.

'I don't see any point, Nicolas. Your life is in New York, or London, or wherever your latest show is being staged. My life is here, in Rocky Creek, with my daughter and my family. We have nothing in common anymore, not even the piano.'

'We have this in common, Serina,' he growled, and in the twinkling of any eye, he captured her startled face in his hands and swooped with his mouth.

No! She might have screamed aloud if she'd been able to scream. But actual screaming was impossible with his lips clamped to hers and his tongue already pushing past her teeth. All she could manage was a low groan, which sounded more like the sound of surrender than any kind of protest.

It was a brutal kiss, punishing and powerful, demanding and devouring, irrefutable and irresistible.

Serina knew, soon after Nicolas started kissing her, that she didn't have a hope in Hades of resisting him. Her body had always had a mind of its own when it came to Nicolas. From the first moment he'd touched her, she'd been his. Whenever they'd made love, he'd evoked feelings in her—both physically and emotionally—that had both consumed and enthralled her. Being with him had quickly become an obsession and an addiction, which only the tyranny of distance had put a halt to. Whenever he'd come home, she'd been there, waiting for him.

So when his head finally lifted, she didn't bother to voice any further protest. She just looked up into his eyes and said breathily, 'All right, Nicolas. You win. I'll go to bed with you one more time. But that will be the end of it,' she added before he could look too triumphant. 'The end of us. There will be no more.'

'Are you quite sure of that, Serina?' he

murmured, his hands turning soft and seductive around her face.

'Quite sure,' she lied in steely tones…

CHAPTER NINE

NICOLAS was taken aback by Serina's tough stance. This wasn't the girl he remembered. She would have just melted into his arms and agreed with whatever he wanted.

But then he remembered the Serina who'd come to him that night at the Opera House. She'd melted all right. For a while. But she'd solidified quickly enough after she'd had what she wanted.

'So it's just sex you want from me again, Serina,' he growled, his fingertips tightening on the soft skin of her flushed cheeks.

Something flickered through her large brown eyes. A momentary shame, perhaps. But she didn't look away. Her gaze stayed steady, and strong.

'That's all you're good for, Nicolas,' came her stunningly hurtful words.

He did his best not to show any visible distress,

finding a slow smile from somewhere. 'If you think insults can save you, Serina, then think again. I haven't come all this way to go home without seeing the way you look when you come. And I will make you beg for it this time, sweetheart.'

Her eyes glittered wildly in return. 'You'll be the one doing the begging, lover,' she spat back at him.

His fingers slid down to caress her throat. 'Is that a challenge?'

'It's a promise.'

His eyes narrowed whilst hot blood rushed along his veins. 'I suggest you ring that daughter of yours and let her know that you won't be home by four,' he snarled.

'And I suggest you stop making suggestions and just drive!'

As Nicolas glowered down into her flushed but feisty face, it came to him that the adult Serina was exciting him much more than the teenage girl ever had. Or even the wildly frustrated creature who'd come to him that night thirteen years ago.

She was a woman now, he saw, more experienced and confident. More...interesting.

He smiled again.

'Excellent idea,' he pronounced, and turned his attention to doing exactly what she'd suggested. Thirty seconds later, he was whizzing along the Oxley Highway, pushing the speed limit to the max as he sped towards their destination.

Serina leant back in the passenger seat and turned her head away to stare blankly through the passenger window.

She'd done it now. Not only had she agreed to have sex with him again, but she'd also challenged him and provoked him.

Nicolas was not the sort of person one challenged, or provoked. As a teenager he'd been one angry young man, with tunnel vision and a quick temper. He'd hated being teased. Hated anyone who told him he couldn't do something. As an adult male, she had no doubt that, down deep, he wouldn't have changed all that much.

But it was too late now. It had been too late the second he leant over and kissed her. There was nothing to do but to go through with what she'd agreed to. Which, of course, she secretly wanted. She wanted it so much she was already trembling inside.

Suddenly, and with typical female thinking, Serina was glad that she'd taken trouble with her appearance today. Glad she'd shaved her legs last night and painted her nails, and worn a pretty set of lingerie under her new dress.

Not that she'd be wearing any of it for long. Nicolas had never been fond of making love under or around clothes. Her accusation earlier that Nicolas was wicked was probably right. But if he was wicked then so was she. She felt wicked now—and terribly turned on.

The next fifteen minutes went agonisingly slowly, despite Nicolas not keeping to the speed limit. Once he reached the outer parts of Port Macquarie, however, the traffic forced him down to sixty, his frustrated mutterings echoing her own feelings.

'I'm not stopping anywhere for lunch,' he growled once he turned the corner that led into the main street of Port. 'I don't want to waste any of the miserably short period of time I have with you.'

Serina said nothing. What was there to say that wasn't shameful?

I don't mind, Nicolas. All I want to eat is you.

'You won't have to starve,' he went on.

'There's wine in the apartment, and fruit and chocolates. I presume you still like chocolates?'

She still didn't speak, or look his way.

'There's no need to sulk,' he snapped. 'You want this as much as I do.'

Her head jerked round, but any smart crack she might have made disappeared once she saw the raw passion in his face. This was the Nicolas she remembered, the Nicolas she'd fallen madly in love with. All of a sudden it seemed stupid to spoil their last time together. If she was going to do this—and it seemed she was—she would do so willingly. But on her terms, not his.

'I won't deny it,' she stated matter-if-factly. 'If I did, you'd find out soon enough I was lying. But let's get one thing straight, Nicolas. This afternoon is our swan song. There will be no encore performance. Once that talent quest is over tomorrow night I want you to leave Rocky Creek and never come back.'

'And what if I don't want to do that?' he retorted. 'I'll have you know I've rented this apartment up here for a week.' And he nodded towards a tall, grey-blue cement-rendered building just ahead on their right that Serina hadn't actually seen before, though she knew of it. Blue Horizon Apartments had opened recently with a big colour spread in the local newspaper.

'I'm sure they'll give you a refund,' she replied as he pulled in to a driveway just to the left of the building.

Once the SUV was stopped in front of the car park security gate, Nicolas glared over at her. 'What gives you the right to make demands like that?'

'I don't have any right,' she admitted. 'But if you do what I ask, I'll do whatever you want for the next four hours. If not, then you can turn around and take me home.'

Nicolas could have called her bluff, the way he had a short time ago. But really, there was no point. All his questions had been answered now. Serina didn't love him anymore. Maybe she'd never loved him. That night thirteen years ago hadn't been about love, it'd been all about lust. As was this afternoon.

She still wanted him. Quite badly, if he was any judge. Which explained why she was so anxious to get rid of him, because she was afraid of what she might do.

Nicolas suspected he could seduce her into going away with him, if he tried hard enough.

But he wasn't that ruthless, despite what she thought of him. He could see that her life here meant the world to her, as did her daughter. To take her away from Rocky Creek would be cruel and truly wicked, which he was not.

Which left him with the harsh reality that this afternoon would be the last time he'd be with her.

Four miserable short hours.

It just wasn't enough.

'Make it six hours,' he counteroffered. 'Call Felicity on her mobile and tell her to go to a friend's place till then.'

'I can't do that. People will talk.'

'Serina, they're going to talk anyway. But if I leave town for good the day after tomorrow, they'll soon forget.'

'If you leave town?'

'That's conditional on your staying with me for six hours. And what was it you offered? Doing whatever I want.'

'That's blackmail!' she protested.

Nicolas laughed. 'No, my darling heart. That's negotiation. So what's it to be?'

'I...I'll ring Felicity later. But not right now. Closer to four.'

'Fine.' Satisfied for the moment, he leant out of the driver's window and swiped the key card across the security unit attached to the wall. As the gate slowly lifted, Nicolas glanced at his watch.

It was noon. High noon.

He smiled a wry smile.

What have I done? Serina agonised when she saw Nicolas smile.

You've sold your soul to the devil, that's what you've done.

No, not my soul. My body. My soul is still mine.

But this last thought was little consolation. Serina's hands curled into tight fists in her lap as Nicolas drove slowly down the ramp before angling the bulky vehicle into an empty parking space in a dimly lit corner of the basement car park. The moment the engine died, a nervous sigh shuddered from her lungs.

'There's no need for that,' he said with surprising tenderness, and reached over to take her tense hands in his. 'I don't mean you any harm, my darling,' he murmured, and lifted her hands to his mouth, where he kissed the whitened knuckles one after the other. 'I just want to make love to you the way I used to. Not what we shared that night at the Opera House. That was way too fast and furious. I want to enjoy you at length the way we did in the beginning. Remember how it used to be between us?'

How could she forget?

Already she was trembling inside.

'You used to do whatever I asked. Whatever I wanted. Be like that with me one more time and I'll leave like you asked me to.'

A soft moan escaped her lips when he uncurled one of her fingers and pushed it deep into his mouth. She closed her eyes as he began to suck, her mind filling with memories of all the things he'd done to her in the past. Nothing had been taboo in the end. Everything had been tried, everything enjoyed. Even…

Serina snapped open at that particular memory.

'You…you do have protection with you, don't you?' she blurted out.

Slowly, his head lifted, leaving her finger wet and tingling.

'Of course,' he said softly.

Of course. Nicolas had always been a thinker and a planner. Only twice had he not practised safe sex with her. That first time. And then during that wildly impassioned encounter at the

Opera House, for which she only had herself to blame.

His head turned at the sound of a group of people walking across the car park and getting in a nearby car.

'Time, I think,' came his oh-so-cool words, 'for us to go upstairs…'

CHAPTER TEN

SERINA'S knees felt like jelly during their short walk to the lift well. She was glad that no one joined them there, leaving them alone for the ride up to Nicolas's floor. She didn't want anyone to see the state she was in. Though nothing much was visible on the outside, nothing except for her possibly haunted eyes and her rock-hard nipples. An outsider could not see her wildly whirling thoughts, or the shocking wetness between her legs.

Nicolas, on the other hand, to all appearances had regained total control of himself. There again, he hadn't touched her since alighting from the SUV, going about his business with the key card in the lift without even glancing her way. So maybe he wasn't quite as cool as he was pretending to be.

Once they left the lift, he did take her elbow, steering her across a grey carpeted foyer and down a corridor to a door marked number seventy-three in silver numbers. A quick swipe of the key card and a green light came on in the silver door handle, Nicolas swiftly pushing the door open.

The apartment was, she saw immediately, not run-of-the-mill holiday accommodation. The living room into which she first walked was very spacious, the décor expensive. The walls and ceilings were painted a soft off-white, with the furniture, floor and accessories in various shades of blue, ranging from the palest of grey-blues to quite bright blues to the darkest navy, with the odd splash of turquoise thrown in.

'Very nice,' she murmured, and dropped her handbag onto a large navy leather armchair before moving across the room to the sliding glass doors, which led out to the balcony.

'It's locked,' she said when the door wouldn't slide open.

Nicolas strode over, lifted the latch then locked it again.

'Oh,' she said, feeling totally flustered and confused.

Nicolas cupped her face and forced her eyes up to his. 'If you think you're going to waste time out there looking at a view you've seen a million times before, Serina, then think again. I didn't bring you up here to play pretend tourist. Now, as pretty as this dress is that you're wearing,' he said, his hands dropping down to the wide belt around her waist, 'it has to go.'

Serina's first instinct was to object. But her second thought was to stay silent and just let him get on with it. After all, this was what she'd agreed to. And what she'd often dreamt about over the years. To somehow be able to go back into the past when they were teenagers and so very much in love.

Which they had been.

Not once had Serina ever felt that the intimacies they'd shared were just acts of lust. It had always been lovemaking, not sex. Nicolas had never made her feel used. Yes, he was dominant and domineering, but he was also tender and loving. He never stopped telling her how much he loved her and how beautiful she was.

Her stomach twisted at this last thought. Would he still think her beautiful? She was not as young, or as firm. She'd had a child. Her breasts drooped a bit and her belly, though without stretch marks, was soft and rounded.

'Nicolas,' she choked out.

His eyes flashed impatience at her. 'What now?'

'Tell me that you love me.'

'What?'

'You don't have to mean it. Just say it. I want to hear you say it.'

Nicolas just stared at her. He would never understand women. Why couldn't she just be honest? She didn't want his love, so why ask for fake words?

'You said you wanted to make love to me the way you used to,' she went on before he could say anything. 'Well, you used to tell me how much you loved me all the time. And how beautiful I was. It made all that we did together…seem right.'

Nicolas was totally unprepared for the wave of emotion that her words evoked. It choked him up, a huge lump forming in his throat.

'You think I'm silly, don't you?' she said in a broken voice, which almost brought him undone.

Somehow he managed to hold himself together, though he had to clear his throat before answering her. His words weren't critical, but his tone was brusque and uncompromising.

'You're a woman, and women look at things differently to men. We don't need the justification of love to make sex acceptable. There's nothing wrong with a man and a woman enjoying each others' bodies. Which we have always done, Serina. More perhaps than most men and women. I can honestly say that I have never forgotten what we shared. It was, indeed, unforgettable. It's why you came to me that night at the Opera House, and why you're here now. Why I'm here. There is a chemistry between us that refuses to die, or even fade. We will take it to our graves. But we're all grown up now,' he said as he removed the belt from her waist and tossed it aside. 'There's no need to say things we don't mean.'

A type of relief claimed Nicolas once he stopped talking and started seriously undressing her. It had taken a supreme effort of will not to say what she wanted him to say. Because, to be brutally honest, he wasn't sure that he did.

Emotions could be deceptive. Especially desire.

He wanted her the way he'd always wanted her. But was that love?

Maybe. Maybe not.

Even if it was, there was no point in loving her. She didn't love him back. He'd overheard what she'd said to her daughter. She'd loved Greg Harmon. She didn't want anything to do with him, except in this most basic way. He'd been right when he said she was just trying to justify her feelings with romantic words. The bottom line was she was here because she wanted sex.

Nicolas's teeth clenched down hard in his jaw, his last thoughts hardening his heart towards her. She wanted sex, did she? Well, he'd give her sex. And he'd make her beg. He hadn't forgotten his earlier threat. If nothing else, he would reduce her to that. And he'd make her say that she loved him.

She'd accused him of coming back for revenge. Who knew? Maybe he had…

CHAPTER ELEVEN

SERINA could not remember Nicolas undressing her quite this quickly before. In the old days he'd liked to take his time over everything. She suspected that their first rushed encounter had seriously embarrassed him, stinging the perfectionist in his nature. But nothing was ever rushed. The undressing, the foreplay, the act itself. He would sometimes spend up to an hour playing with her body's erogenous zones, using his hands mostly, but also his mouth. He'd loved making her climax over and over before he entered her, loved watching her eyes, loved the feel of her wet heat when his own flesh finally fused with hers.

She knew all this because he would tell her, his constant stream of hot words turning her on, and keeping her turned on.

Even that fateful night thirteen years ago, when they'd fallen upon each other like wild beasts, he'd talked incessantly, telling her how much he'd missed her; how much he loved her. He'd only become silent when he fell asleep.

Today he was stripping her in total silence, almost roughly, not bothering to linger as he once would have. In no time she was nude before him, trembling with nerves and tension.

He stepped back at that stage and just looked at her, his eyes both hot and cold at the same time. Serina had no idea what he was thinking. He seemed angry for some reason, which upset her.

'What is it, Nicolas?' she blurted out. 'What's wrong?'

'Why should anything be wrong?' he snapped and reefed his shirt out of the waist-band of his trousers.

Suddenly she understood. He'd come all this way, hoping that they could find each other again. Maybe he'd even hoped she would finally go away with him. One afternoon of reliving old times was not what he had in mind.

Her heart twisted with dismay. *Oh, Nicolas, Nicolas, why didn't you come back for me sooner? Why did you wait till it was too late?*

But at least he'd come. She had that to be grateful for. She would not die without knowing that she'd meant as much to him as he had to her.

'Let me do that,' she said softly when he started wrenching open the buttons on his shirt.

As she stepped forward to take his hands away, she gazed up into his undeniably startled eyes. 'I always wanted to undress you. But you never would let me. You might find you like it.' She started slowly undoing his shirt buttons one by one, satisfied when she heard his breath catch in his throat.

It was exciting, taking control, something she'd never done, either with Nicolas or with Greg. Her husband had been a conventional lover with simple sexual needs and definite expectations of her as his wife. He'd interpreted her initial reluctance to sleep with him as an indication that sex was not a high priority with her. Serina had never led him to believe otherwise. She rarely said no to him when he approached her in their marital bed. But the pleasure he gave her, whilst pleasant enough, never came even close to what she'd experienced with Nicolas, which she knew she would experience today. Already her heart was racing with anticipation of what lay ahead.

* * *

Nicolas could not believe he was doing this, letting her undress him. It was not his usual modus operandi when it came to sex. There was, however, affection in Serina's lovely dark eyes as she undid the buttons on his shirt. Seeing that affection stirred both his body and his soul. It was no use. He couldn't pretend this was just about sex. Maybe it was for Serina. She'd obviously come a long way in experience over the years. As much as it killed him to admit it, Greg Harmon had obviously been an excellent lover. Nicolas couldn't imagine Serina falling in love with any man who didn't please her sexually.

But Greg Harmon is dead, he reminded himself in his usual pragmatic and rather ruthless fashion, *and I'm here!*

No way was Nicolas going to let jealousy ruin the next few hours. Serina was his again, for now. And he was going to enjoy her to the full.

'You've looked after yourself, haven't you?' she said admiringly when she finally pushed his shirt back off his shoulders.

He had. Not because he was obsessed by his body image, but because he'd found working out was an antidote for the depression that had seized him after the accident. After a while, going to the gym several times a week had become a habit. He was glad now that he had, glad that she could look at him and like what she saw. He certainly liked what he saw. Serina was even more beautiful for having had a child. Her body was curvier and sexier. *She* was sexier.

'I always loved it that you didn't have much body hair,' she murmured as she ran her fingertips provocatively over his smooth chest muscles. His nipples tightened under her touch. It wasn't the only physical change she was evoking. He'd thought his flesh couldn't become harder. But he was wrong.

'Serina,' he bit out warningly.

'Mmmm?'

'Move on,' he advised thickly.

She smiled. It was a woman's smile, sweet and sexy at the same time.

When her hands dropped to the waistband of his trousers, Nicolas had to use all of his will-power to take control of his body.

He managed to get through her undressing him without disaster striking. But the moment her hand reached out to touch him down there, he simply had to stop her.

'No,' he growled, and grabbed her hand in his.

Serina stared up at him, her dark eyes startled.

'You only have yourself to blame,' he said drily as he scooped her up into his arms and carried her into the bedroom. 'You are way too beautiful to last long this first time.'

She didn't say anything, just gave him a look that implied he was lying. Which he wasn't, of course.

'But never fear, my darling,' he went on as he laid her down on top of the soft blue quilt. 'Things won't always be this rushed.'

'You're…you're not wearing protection?' she sputtered when he went to join her on the bed.

His teeth clenched down hard in his jaw with frustration. 'See? I've totally lost my head over my desire for you. Won't be long.' And he walked off in the direction of the en suite bathroom.

Serina just lay there, staring after him and wondering if he'd deliberately tried to have sex with her without a condom.

Surely not! But if not, then what? The thought that he had been overcome with desire for her was flattering in the extreme.

Don't go there, Serina, she warned herself. *He does not love you. This is all about winning, not love.*

He came striding back into the bedroom, looking like a Viking warrior intent on ravagement. The sight of his intense desire inflamed her own once more, making her belly tighten and her thighs tremble. Suddenly, it didn't matter why he'd come back. He was here: her Nicolas, her one true love.

'Nicolas,' she choked out, holding out her arms and opening her legs at the same time.

He groaned, then fell upon her, much like he had that night at the Opera House, his flesh fusing with hers like a sword being slid roughly into its scabbard. She gasped and clung to him, her arms wrapping around his back, her legs lifting to wind tightly around his waist. She whimpered as he surged into her again and again, her head threshing from side to side.

'No, don't,' he said with a groan when she went to shut her eyes. 'Look at me, Serina, look at me.'

So she looked at him, and came immediately, her mouth falling open as she sucked in some much-needed air. He kissed her then, kissed her and came at the same time, without missing a beat of his merciless rhythm, Serina wallowing in the pleasure and power of his twin possessions, thrilling to the way her body responded to both. She would have stayed that way forever, if it were possible.

But his climax finally ended and his head finally lifted.

She stared up at him as he stroked her hair back from her sweat-beaded forehead, her eyes searching his face as she tried to read his mind. But nothing of his inner feelings showed on his face this time. The stormy passion she'd glimpsed earlier had obviously been sated, at least temporarily.

'I feel a lot better now,' he said. 'Don't you? No, you don't have to answer that. I felt your climax right down to my toes. You have to admit that some things never change, my darling. You still come quicker than any girl I've ever been with.'

Her heart curled over in dismay that he could be so cold and cruel whilst he was still inside her. But it was good, in a way, for him to show his true colours. It would stop her from harbouring silly thoughts, the kind that had filled her soul when she'd held out her arms to him.

'I'm rather hungry,' he went on in that coolly casual fashion that she was sure she would soon hate. 'I dare say you are, too. Time I think, for some refreshments. And perhaps some refreshing. Good thinking, Nicolas,' he said, and withdrew from her body with such abruptness that she gasped.

He smiled down into her bereft face.

'Sorry, darling heart,' he said, patting her patronisingly on the cheek. 'But needs must. Once I have the spa bath full and all our goodies lined up in there, it will be all systems go again. Meanwhile, let me tell you again how beautiful you are.'

'Don't say that!' she snapped. 'You don't mean it. I know you don't.'

His smile, when it came, was extremely sardonic. 'I'm saying it to make all that we're going to do this afternoon seem right.'

Suddenly, she was afraid. Of this cold, cruel Nicolas, but mostly of herself. Because she was still turned on by him. Even now. 'What...what are we going to do?'

Sexy blue eyes glittered down into her.

'Whatever I want you to do,' he said. 'That was the deal, wasn't it...?'

CHAPTER TWELVE

'ANOTHER chocolate, my sweet,' he said, and leant forward to pop one of the deliciously creamy delicacies into her mouth.

No point in objecting, Serina thought. No point in objecting to anything he suggested. The bitter truth was she simply didn't have the will-power to resist him, or the desire.

Besides, she was ravenously hungry, having not eaten a thing since a very light breakfast— just coffee and one slice of toast.

So she ate the chocolate and washed it down with a mouthful of champagne, all the while wondering why he hadn't suggested something more decadent than their current positions in the spa bath. They were sitting at opposite ends, only their feet touching occasionally.

It was not what Serina had envisioned. What she had, perhaps, secretly hoped for.

This wasn't the first time they'd shared a bath.

In the old days he would have placed her across his lap, his swollen sex deep inside of her whilst they lay back in the water like two spoons. His hands would have covered her breasts and he would be whispering hot words of love and passion into her ears.

'What time is it, do you think?' she asked suddenly.

'Haven't got my watch on,' he replied. 'But my guess is it's just after one. Plenty of time left. We could even waste a little of it talking.'

'Talking?' she echoed in startled tones.

'You don't want to talk? Too bad, Serina. It's not your choice. So tell me, was your marriage happy?'

The last thing she wanted to talk about was her marriage. Serina sipped some more champagne in an effort to find composure.

'Like most marriages,' she said at last, not quite meeting his probing gaze, 'it had its ups and downs. But on the whole we were happy.'

His head tipped slightly to one side in that way people did when they were trying to detect if someone was lying to them.

'Why only one child?' he went on, blue eyes boring into her.

Serina's stomach tightened, but she managed a nonchalant shrug. 'We tried for more. It just didn't happen.'

'Your fault or his?'

'Neither. We were perfectly healthy, the doctors said.' Now this was not totally true. Greg had discovered quite a few years back that he had a low sperm count, possibly because he'd had mumps as an adolescent. Technically, he had been still capable of fathering a child, but conceiving had not been easy.

'I see,' Nicolas said. 'Well at least you have Felicity. She's a delightful child.'

'Delightful,' Serina agreed. 'But difficult.'

Nicolas smiled an indulgent smile. 'Yes. I can see that she might be that.'

Serina knew she had to get off that topic and quick.

'And what of you, Nicolas?' she countered. 'Have you anyone waiting for you back in New York? That pretty little Japanese violinist perhaps.'

His eyebrows lifted. 'You know about Junko?'

So he was sleeping with her!

'I know of her. Felicity did an Internet search

and showed me what you'd been up to over the years.'

'I see.'

'You've had a lot of beautiful women, by all accounts.'

'True,' came his cool reply.

Dear heaven, but he was annoying.

'You never wanted to marry any of them?'

'Yes. Once. But it didn't work out.'

'When was that?'

'Years ago,' he responded nonchalantly, as though it was of no importance. 'Look, I can see that making idle chitchat is not our forte. Not this afternoon, anyway. Let's get out of this bath and back to what we do best together.'

He rose up through the water, soapy bubbles clinging to various parts of his body—his shoulders his chest…

She stared up at it, then up at him.

'As you can see,' he said drily as he stepped out of the bath and reached for a towel, 'I have recovered sufficiently to continue. Now put down that champagne, beautiful. I need someone out here to dry me, someone who knows just how I like it done.'

Serina's heartbeat quickened at his command,

her head whirling with hot jabs of desire. At last it was going to begin again. At last, she could touch him as she'd been dying to touch him.

Foolish man, Nicolas was to think thirty seconds later. She didn't dry herself at all, her beautiful body glistening with moisture as she proceeded to dry him, slowly, sensuously, dabbing at his arms, shoulders and back, then moving around to press the towel against his buttocks before slowly running it down the back of his legs. His gut tightened when she began to move the towel up between his legs.

'Delay,' he'd read in the last chapter of an old sex manual he'd once bought, 'is the best way to increase the intensity of one's climax.'

Serina had obviously learned that lesson well. She pulled the towel away and walked round to face him. There, she stood before him and rubbed the towel slowly over her own body, her dilated eyes showing him that she was just as turned on as he was.

'Throw the towel away,' he groaned.

She did.

'Kneel down.'

She obeyed once more. Without question, without hesitating.

'Now tell me that you love me.'

Her head tipped backwards as her eyes flew up to his.

'You don't have to mean it,' he ground out, his hands reaching to tug her hair down from where she'd wound it up on top of her head, out of the reach of the bath water. 'Just say it. So that it makes what you're going to do seem right.'

'Nicolas, don't,' she croaked out.

'Don't what, my darling?' His fingers splayed through her hair, spreading it out onto her shoulders. 'Don't humiliate you this way? How can it possibly be humiliation when you want this as much as I do?'

Her sob filled him with self-loathing. But nothing was going to stop him. Not her distress, or his conscience.

'No one has ever done it better than you, Serina,' he crooned.

When her head drooped and her hands lifted from her sides, he thought she was about to burst into tears. Instead, she reached up and touched him, enfolding delicate fingers around his aching penis and pressing the tip against her lips.

His whole body shuddered as though lightning had struck it. She didn't stop there, however.

She opened those soft sweet lips and took him into the wet heat of her mouth. He stared down at her as her head lifted and fell in a slow but merciless rhythm. He wanted to cry out, to scream. He wanted, more than anything, to hate her.

And he did hate her in that moment when he knew he could no longer contain his desire. For as his body raced towards a climax, the victory suddenly felt like hers. She was the one in control here. She was the one doing the using and the rejecting once again.

Serina wanted him gone from her life. And she was prepared to do anything—even this— to achieve her goal.

Such thoughts brought bitterness and a dark desire, not to witness his own ragged release, but hers. She was the one he wanted to see out of control. Had he forgotten his threat to make her beg? He was hardly achieving that this way.

At the last moment he found the strength to pull free of her, glorying in the glazed and confused eyes she raised up to his face.

'I'll take a raincheck on that, my love,' he said as he lifted her onto unsteady feet. 'I have other things in mind for this afternoon. And for you…'

CHAPTER THIRTEEN

NICOLAS shook his head ruefully as he gazed down at Serina's sleeping form. So much for his intention to indulge in a whole afternoon of vengeful sex, where she'd have lost control and begged for mercy.

If only he hadn't brought her back to bed.

The bed had been a mistake, as had his unsuccessful attempt to arouse her so much with his own mouth that she'd plead for release. She'd been aroused all right, he was pretty sure of that. But not as much as he had been. Before he knew it he was reaching for another condom. Even worse, he'd taken her in the spoon position, which meant he hadn't even been able to see her face when she came. If she had, that is. Men could never be too sure about such things, he'd discovered over the years. All in all, things hadn't gone according to plan. Afterwards, she'd fallen asleep.

A glance at his watch showed it was just on three. Of course he could wake her up and start all over again, this time reliving a few of the more erotic foreplays and positions that they'd explored at length all those years ago.

The possibilities were endless. But he just didn't want to. He didn't want to feel what he felt every time he touched her.

It wasn't hate at all.

Nicolas knew that he could not face another three hours of this emotional torment. It was time to call a halt before his thoughts and feelings got the better of him.

'You're a sad case, Nick, my man,' he muttered to himself as he rose from the rumpled bed and headed for the bathroom.

Five minutes later, a dressed Nicolas was shaking Serina's right shoulder.

She moaned softly, rolling over onto her back and stretching voluptuously before blinking open her eyes.

Nicolas was glad he was fully dressed. His body was still, unfortunately, on a different wavelength to his mind.

'Time for me to take you home, sweetheart,' he said, his voice as hard as his poor tormented flesh.

She blinked and sat up, her full breasts moving in a most provocative way. 'What?'

'You heard me. It's time for me to take you home.'

Alarm filled her face. 'It's six o'clock already? Why didn't you wake me? Oh no, I didn't ring Felicity.' She glanced at the digital bedside clock before throwing him a confused look. 'But… but…it's only just after three o'clock!'

'I've changed my mind about the length of this afternoon's activities,' he interrupted in a cold, crisp voice. 'I've had enough.'

'Enough?' she echoed rather blankly.

'Did I not make myself clear? Then let me put it another way. You're still one heck of a good lay, but I can see that you were right. Our relationship, such as it was, is dead in the water. All that was left was some lingering flames. This afternoon snuffed out the last of those flames, good and proper. For which I am grateful. Now I can go back to my life the day after tomorrow and not give you a second thought. And you, my love, will surely do the same.'

Serina was grateful that he turned away from her at that point. For her face had to have betrayed her shock at this last statement.

Not give him a second thought?

Was he insane, or just seriously deluded?

'Better shake a leg,' he said over his shoulder as he strode from the bedroom in the direction of the living room.

She stumbled out of the bed, only then realising that her clothes were out in the living room. Where he was.

To walk out there naked after what he'd just said sent a shiver running down her spine. Not once, in the past, had Nicolas referred to her as a 'lay', either good or otherwise. The word was repulsive in her eyes. Didn't he know how much she still loved him? Hadn't he felt the love in her lips? In her willingness to do whatever he wanted?

Of course not. Why would he? She'd acted like a tough cookie on the way here, saying that sex was all he was good for. She only had herself to blame for the way he was treating her.

But, oh…it had been wonderful for a short while. She'd been able to pretend that nothing had changed, that they were young lovers again, where nothing existed for her but the heat of the moment. She'd wallowed in the thrill of obeying his commands; in playing the role of his love slave.

But the time for pretence was over now, she realised as a bleak dismay filled her heart. It was time to go back to the real world and her real life. Time, too, to get a grip.

Gathering herself, she hurried into the bathroom, where she grabbed a towel and was wrapping it tightly around her nakedness when she caught a glimpse of her reflection in the vanity mirror.

Goodness, she could not go back to the office looking like that! Her hair was a mess, her lips looked puffy and her eyes…

If eyes were the windows to one's soul, then her soul was in big trouble!

Steeling herself once more, she hurried out to the living room where she found Nicolas making himself a cup of coffee in the kitchen. Ignoring his sharp, top-to-toe glance, she set about scooping up her clothes from the floor. Finally, and without a single word, she snatched up her handbag as well and bolted back to the bathroom.

Serina had just made herself look respectable when her mobile phone rang. She stiffened before rifling the handset out of the bottom of her bag and whisking it to her ear. Since the terrible call about Greg's death, she experienced a rush of anxiety whenever her mobile rang at odd times. Felicity knew not to ring her on it unless there was an emergency. But who else could it be?

'Yes?'

'It's only me, Serina,' her mother replied somewhat wearily. 'Not Felicity. You have to stop worrying about that child, dear. She's extremely capable of looking after herself.'

'Yes, Mum. I do know that. So what's up? It's not like you to ring me on this phone.'

'I tried the office number but it was engaged. That's why I rang you on your mobile. I thought you might like to know how things went with Mrs Johnson today.'

'Oh, yes, yes, I would. But can you tell me quickly? I'm still in Port Macquarie, and I told Felicity I'd be home by four.'

'What are you doing in Port?'

Serina swallowed. 'Having lunch with you know who.'

'Who? Oh, you mean Nicolas Dupre. Really? I'm surprised. I got the impression you weren't too pleased with Felicity for securing his services as judge for the talent quest.'

'I wasn't. And I didn't want to have lunch with him, believe me,' she said. 'But he asked me in front of those silly girls in my office and they made it impossible for me to refuse.'

'You're right. They are silly, those two. But nice girls all the same. So what's he like these days? Still handsome, I would expect.'

'Mum, could this conversation wait till later? I'm running out of time and I can't talk whilst I drive.' It seemed wise to let her mother think she had her own wheels.

'It will have to be much later. I haven't left Newcastle yet.'

'So how is Mrs Johnson?'

'Healthy as a horse. The doc gave her some mild blood pressure pills and told her to lay off the sherry.'

'Which she won't.'

'I doubt it. Anyway, dear, off you go and I'll ring you when I get home.'

'Please do.' And she hung up.

'Who were you talking to in here?' Nicolas said as he flung open the door.

'My mother,' she replied brusquely, and dropped the phone back into her bag. 'She rang to let me know how Mrs Johnson is.'

'And?'

'She'll live till she's a hundred. Now, if you don't mind, I need to get back to Rocky Creek.'

'You're the one who's been taking your time. Let's go.'

The drive back to Rocky Creek was excruciating. Neither of them spoke, not a single word.

Serina stared through the passenger window and tried not think about what she'd just done. If her mother ever found out she'd jumped into bed with Nicolas within hours of his returning, she would not believe her. Of course, her mother never knew about the highly sexual nature of their teenage affair. She probably thought her dear darling daughter had gone to her wedding night a virgin.

Serina would have liked to confide in her mother. To confess everything. But she couldn't. Her mother would not understand. She would be totally shocked, and bitterly ashamed.

I'll have to do what I've always done, Serina thought wearily. *Keep my mouth shut and all my dark dirty secrets to myself.*

Just after they'd gone through Wauchope, Nicolas's own brooding silence began to seriously bother her. If he considered their relationship dusted and dried, as he'd claimed, then why was he so angry with her?

And he was. She could feel his anger hitting her in waves.

They were just coming down the hill towards the bridge that crossed Rocky Creek when she decided to speak up.

'There's no need for this, Nicolas,' she said with more calm than she was feeling. 'It's childish.'

'What's childish?'

'Giving me the cold-shoulder treatment. Look, I'm sorry if things haven't worked out the way you might have imagined. I'm sorry I'm not the girl you remember. Like I said, things change. So do people.'

His sidewards glance showed a reluctant flash of admiration. 'You've certainly grown up a lot.'

'Marriage and motherhood has a tendency to do that.'

'Are you saying I haven't grown up?'

'Not at all. But parenthood has a way of forcing a person into early maturity, and into being less selfish.'

'Ah, so you're saying that I'm selfish.'

'Don't put words into my mouth, Nicolas. You

would know better than me if you're selfish or not.'

Nicolas nodded. 'I suspect that I am. My mother always said I was.'

They both fell silent again as he drove into town. Despite knowing she would see Nicolas again the next day, Serina didn't want this day to end badly.

'Can't we part friends, Nicolas?' she asked, her voice cracking a little.

He did not reply at first. But then he nodded. 'If that's what you want.'

Oh, yes, of course it wasn't what she wanted. But what she wanted—what she'd always wanted—just couldn't be. She'd made her bed all those years ago. And now she had to lie in it, till the end of her days.

'It's what I want,' she said.

He pulled into the car park of Brown's Landscaping and Building Supplies, but didn't bother to park, just drove straight up to the front door. The face he turned towards her was totally unreadable.

'Friends, then,' he said, and bent to give her a peck on the cheek. 'See you tomorrow.'

Her eyes met his for a long moment. She almost said it.

I love you.

I've always loved you.

But only almost.

When tears pricked at her eyes, she did the only thing she could do. She smiled, then got out of the car and waved him off.

She didn't go into the office. She could not bear to make conversation right at that moment, couldn't bear any more pretending. She went straight to her own car and drove straight home.

Felicity wasn't there yet, thank heavens. Her daughter wasn't renowned for punctuality. Just as well, because by then serious tears were threatening. Serina just managed to get herself inside before the floodgates opened.

'Oh, Nicolas,' she cried as she sank down to the floor, her back against the front door, her head dropping into her hands. 'Why did you have to come back?'

An equally distraught Nicolas was thinking exactly the same thing as he drove back to Port Macquarie. If he hadn't promised Felicity to judge that stupid bloody talent quest tomorrow he would have taken the first available flight back to Sydney. He didn't want to see Serina again. He didn't want to have to pretend to everyone that they were just 'good friends'. His life had been much easier when she was just a memory, one which had occasionally tormented him but which he'd been able to put aside, most of the time.

Impossible to put aside a flesh-and-blood woman in the same room as him, one who only a short time earlier had been kneeling, naked, before him.

Nicolas shuddered.

He had to stop thinking about that. Had to stop thinking that he'd never meant anything more to her than just a piece of meat.

But she'd said as much, hadn't she?

Sex is all you're good for, Nicolas.

They were her very own words.

She'd also said he was childish. And selfish.

As Nicolas drove back to Port Macquarie, he mulled over everything she'd said and done that day. By the time he let himself back into his apartment he'd come to the conclusion that Serina was right. He was childish and selfish. And extremely egotistical to think she might still love him. Which of course was what had brought him here in the first place. That vain hope.

Very vain.

It saddened him to face the truth, but it had to be faced. He'd lost his chance with Serina twenty years ago. That episode at the Opera House had meant no more to her than a one-night stand. As had this afternoon.

Opening one of the wine bottles, Nicolas poured himself a long glass and sat down to drink. Think of tomorrow as a job, he lectured himself. A series of auditions for a show. He'd always liked auditions. Liked the anticipation of discovering someone with real talent. Who knew? Maybe someone in Rocky Creek primary school has real talent…

CHAPTER FOURTEEN

NICOLAS sat down at the judge's table and kept his eyes glued to the stage. That way he wouldn't be tempted to look over at Serina, whom he knew was sitting in the first row of seats, a little to his left. He'd managed to avoid her in the main, although even a short hello and a few miserable glimpses had burned her appearance into his poor besotted brain.

She was wearing white, pure virginal white. Unfortunately, she looked anything but, her dress being halter-necked with a deep V neckline, a tightly belted waist and a gathered shirt that emphasised her hourglass figure and gave rise to the kind of erotic thoughts she always evoked in him.

Felicity walking onto the stage was a good distraction. He hadn't forgotten that she was going to play at some stage this afternoon and he was really looking forward to it, though he rather suspected Mrs Johnson's effusive praise earlier over Felicity's abilities as a pianist might be exaggerated.

'Reminds me of you, Nicolas,' the old lady had said.

Unlikely, given Felicity was a girl and only twelve. Although she looked older standing there in a pale blue dress and shoes that had heels. Her long dark hair swung around her slender shoulders the way Serina's did when she walked. She was, however, taller than her mother. There again, her father had been tall.

'Act number one,' Felicity announced into the microphone, 'will be Jonathon Clarke. Jonathon is in fourth grade and he's going to juggle. Jonathon?' She waved towards the wings and a skinny, nervous-looking boy with short brown hair and glasses emerged. Some taped music started, but Jonathon didn't. Whoever was behind the scenes stopped the tape, then started again.

Nicolas had a feeling that he wasn't seeing the winner.

Rocky Creek Primary School didn't have a great deal of talent, Nicolas accepted by the time he'd sat through eight very mediocre acts. But what the kids lacked in talent they made up for in enthusiasm. There was a real buzz in the hall, which was full to the brim with parents, locals and some concert-goers not so local.

None of them seemed disappointed with the acts so far, applauding wildly at the end of each. Nicolas, who appreciated he'd been spoiled by years of seeing top performers all over the world, put aside his super-critic hat and kept his comments on the kind and constructive side. The audience seemed appreciative of his ability to find praise for even the worst performance.

So far he'd endured the hapless Jonathon, who'd dropped more clubs than he caught; a gymnastic-style dance troop of fifth-grade girls whose movements often got out of sync; a poetry reading of 'The Man From Snow River', complete with stick horses thundering across the stage in the background; two separate country and western singers with absolutely no originality; a twelve-year-old magician whose magic was straight out of a do-it-yourself manual; an Elvis impersonator, who'd been hilarious, because he was so atrocious. And last but not least, a ten-year-old boy named Cory, playing the spoons.

Actually, he wasn't half-bad. If no one better came along, Nicolas was going to give Cory first prize.

Only two to go, according to the program. A twelve-year-old hip-hop dancer named Kirsty. And an eleven-year-old girl—her name was Isabella—singing 'Danny Boy'.

He should have known 'Danny Boy' would get in there somewhere.

Kirsty was somewhat of a pleasant surprise. She was darned good. But Isabella was clearly the star act of the night, the audience falling silent the moment she opened her mouth, her voice as pure and as clear as a bell.

Everyone clapped wildly when she finished, Nicolas included. He didn't have to think too hard over who would win, or who would be runner-up. He'd make that second prize a dead heat between Kirsty, the hip-hop dancer, and Cory, the spoon boy. It would be simple to add a bit of money to the prize pool himself, if need be.

But before any of this could happen, however, there was one event left: Felicity's special performance.

Nicolas found his heartbeat quickening when she walked back out onto the stage.

Surely he couldn't be nervous for her.

But he was, nervous as hell.

Nicolas had never been nervous himself before a performance. He used to be excited. He could not wait to get out there, to show what he could do, to blow his audience away with his brilliance.

But then he'd always been super confident when it came to playing the piano. Girls—especially young girls like Felicity—rarely possessed that kind of confidence.

Yet as he watched her cross to the centre of the stage, there was no hesitation in her stride. She stopped there for a moment, faced the audience and bowed, at the same time throwing him a smile that wasn't just confident. It was super confident.

'Wait till you hear this,' Felicity's principal whispered from where he was sitting beside Nicolas at the judge's table. 'Felicity would have won hands down if she'd entered, you know.'

It was a telling remark, coming so soon after Isabella's almost faultless rendition of 'Danny Boy'.

Nicolas watched, his mouth drying as Felicity moved over to the piano that had not been used as yet that night, Isabella having sung unaccompanied and the dancers using recorded music.

Another smile came his way after she sat down on the stool and lifted her hands to the keys.

'I have chosen to play this medley of pieces in honour of our very special guest here tonight,' she said to the audience. 'I cannot hope to play them as well as he once did. But I will do my best and hope he forgives my mistakes.'

What mistakes? Nicolas was to think numbly thirty seconds later as Felicity's fingers flew over the keys. He'd never heard Rimsky-Korsakov's 'Flight of the Bumblebee' performed any better by one so young. In no time the fast, flashy piece was over, Felicity switching with effortless ease and surprising sensitivity into the haunting adagio from Beethoven's 'Moonlight Sonata'. Lastly, just as everyone in the audience was almost in tears, she launched into Chopin's very showy polonaise 'Heroic', a piece requiring great technical brilliance and showmanship.

Chopin was a favourite choice of composer amongst concert pianists, especially his polonaises. This particular one had been a staple of Nicolas's list. He watched, totally amazed, as Felicity attacked the wild sweep of notes with the same kind of panache and passion that he'd possessed, which the critics had loved. She never looked up at any sheets of music because there were none there. She was playing from memory as he'd always done.

Nicolas could not believe it. Only twelve and already she could play like this. Why, she could take the world by storm in a few years!

Felicity finished the polonaise with a flourish, bending over the keys in a long, dramatic pause before slowly lifting her hands. She tossed her hair back from her shoulders as she stood up, taking her time to turn and bow to the audience, all the while with a 'Yes, I know I'm good' expression on her face.

It was then that she broke into a grin and winked at him.

The cheeky minx, Nicolas thought as he jumped to his feet, clapping and shouting 'Bravo!' as European audiences sometimes did. Everyone else in the hall started doing likewise and Felicity finally began to look a little embarrassed. It was left to the principal of the school to hurry up onto the stage and bring some order back into proceedings.

'Wasn't that just wonderful, folks?' he said,

and gave a by then embarrassed-looking Felicity a shoulder squeeze. 'Not only is our school captain a great little pianist, but she's also a great little organiser. We have her to thank for the presence here tonight of our esteemed guest and judge, Mr Nicolas Dupre. For anyone who doesn't know, Mr Dupre was Australia's most famous concert pianist till a tragic accident cut short his career a decade ago. But you can't keep a Rocky Creek lad down for long. He then went on to become an equally famous theatrical entrepreneur. Some of you might have seen the segment about him on TV a few years ago. Anyway, we are most grateful that he found the time to be with us here tonight. He came a long way. Now...we come to the most important part of the evening. Will Mr Dupre please come up onto the stage and announce the winners?'

Nicolas rose, and made his way forward to some ear-splitting applause.

Serina wasn't clapping, however, her hands twisting in her lap as she watched Nicolas mount the short flight of steps then walk across the stage to where Felicity and Fred Tarleton were standing.

He looked magnificent, dressed in a charcoal-grey suit which must have cost a small fortune. Not only did it fit his body to perfection, but there also wasn't a single wrinkle where the sleeves met his broad shoulders. His shirt was blue, about the same colour as his eyes. His tie was dark blue and grey striped. Only his collar-length blond hair spoiled his image as a millionaire businessman. That, and the inherent sensuality in his face.

Serina heard a few soft sighs from the women in the audience.

In a way, those sounds provided a degree of comfort. How could she blame herself for being besotted by the man when perfect strangers were affected by him?

But it wasn't his sex appeal that was causing her hands to be wrung. Or her stomach to be hopelessly in knots. It was the fear that he might have seen the truth during Felicity's astounding performance just now.

Surely he must have seen what was so obvious to her. That this was his own flesh and blood playing up there. His genes, not Greg's.

She leant forward in her seat to get a closer look at the expression on his face when he approached Felicity. When his daughter smiled up at him, he smiled back, just as happily, without hesitation, without even a hint of distress or anger.

He hadn't seen! He didn't even suspect!

Perversely, any relief Serina felt was tinged by a bitter resentment. What was it about men that they had no sensitivity, or intuition? He should have seen what was obvious. But no, they only saw what they wanted to see. Or what their male ego let them see, and believe.

Nicolas had believed she didn't love him all those years ago, and he believed it once again today. Yet she'd shown him in that bedroom this afternoon how much she did.

She shook her head and sank back into her seat.

'He hasn't changed much,' Mrs Johnson said from where she was sitting on the right side of Serina.

'No,' Serina agreed with considerable irony. He was still a blind fool!

'Hush up, you two,' her mother said impatiently from the other side of Serina.

Nicolas took the microphone from Fred Tarleton and faced the audience.

'Firstly,' he said, 'my heartiest congratulations,

Felicity, for what was, indeed, a spectacular performance. I know I could not have done better myself at your age. Such prodigious talent is a tribute to the dedication and skill of her teacher, Mrs Johnson, who was my own first teacher. Mrs Johnson…' He bowed gallantly towards the old lady. 'I salute you.'

'I take that back,' Mrs Johnson murmured. 'He has changed. The boy I taught had no charm whatsoever.'

A swift sidewards glance showed Serina the old lady was preening under his praise and that well-learned charm.

Her teeth clenched down hard in her jaw.

She sat there, silently fuming—which was insane!—as he went through the process of allotting the prizes, exerting more of his charm and gaining more approval from the audience as he awarded not one but two runner-up prizes. It had been a foregone conclusion that once Felicity was out of the running that Isabella would win. Not that Serina minded that. Isabella was a delightful girl with a truly lovely voice.

Serina tried telling herself she should be grateful that Nicolas hadn't twigged to the truth. Possibly she would be, in time.

Just not right now!

'I have one last presentation to make before today's event comes to a close,' Nicolas said, everyone in the hall falling silent and snapping to attention. 'Felicity, I think you should be the one to receive this.' And he extracted from the breast pocket of his suit jacket what looked like a cheque. 'It was your lovely letter that brought me here. A touching letter, folks, about her dad's tragic death in the Victorian bushfires. As you all know, this afternoon was a fund-raiser for the local bushfire brigade of which her dad was president. Now as much as you have all turned out in wonderful numbers and paid your money at the door, I made enquires about what it would cost to buy just one of those new firefighting trucks that Felicity told me about and I don't think you're going to make it today, not unless I give things a helping hand. So here you are, dear girl. I think it should be enough.'

Serina watched her daughter's eyes widen as she stared at the cheque, watched her daughter then throw her arms around Nicolas. By the time Nicolas disengaged her, Felicity's big brown eyes were dancing with happiness.

'It's for three hundred thousand dollars!' she shouted to everyone.

Everyone began to clap. Everyone, that is, but Serina, who was crying. Her mother put an arm around her shoulders.

'There there, love. I know. It's still hard. But I'm sure Greg must be happy tonight, looking down at his daughter from heaven. Happy and proud.'

Serina cried all the harder…

CHAPTER FIFTEEN

THE after-concert party was in full swing, with Nicolas being bombarded with both finger food and conversation. People kept coming up to him to congratulate him on a job well done and to say thank you, the girls from Serina's office included—though not Serina, he noted ruefully. She kept her distance, even when her own mother and Mrs Johnson were chatting to him.

Felicity brought along her paternal grandparents, Franny and Bert Harmon, whom he'd never met before. They looked like they were in their late seventies and rather an odd couple: Bert was tall and thin whilst Franny was very short and plump. But both of them had grey hair and dark, gentle eyes.

'Nanna and Pop bought your old house, you know,' Felicity said after she'd introduced them.

'Really?'

'And your old piano. That's what I first learned to play on.'

Nicolas was quite startled by this news. He'd imagined that her having piano lessons had been Serina's doing, that Felicity would have learned to play on her mother's piano. Serina had had her own instrument long before Nicolas acquired his, courtesy of a competition he'd won. Till then he'd always practised on Mrs Johnson's piano.

'Whenever I went to stay at Nanna and Pop's,' Felicity went on, 'I could hear the kids having lessons next door at Mrs Johnson's. Her music room was just over the fence from my bedroom window. I used to love to lie in bed and listen.'

Nicolas could hardly believe what he was hearing. Talk about coincidence!

'Then, one day, when I was about three,' Felicity continued, 'I can't actually remember this…but Pop tells me he came downstairs and I was trying to play. He decided then and there I should have lessons. To tell the truth, Mum wasn't all that keen but Dad was, even though he wasn't musical at all.'

'Tone deaf Greg was,' Franny said with a nod. 'But he was so proud of you, love. I'm sure he would have been very proud of you tonight. The way you played. Nicolas was right. You were quite magnificent.'

'If you moved to Sydney to attend the conservatorium of music,' Nicolas said to her, 'you would become an even better pianist. In a few years, you could be giving concerts all over the world.'

Felicity looked very taken aback. 'But I would hate that,' she said very forthrightly. 'I love playing the piano, Nicolas, but I don't want to do it for a living. Good heavens, no! I'm going to become a vet.'

'A vet,' he echoed blankly.

'Golly, yes. Who'd want to be a concert pianist?' she went on with the tactlessness of youth. 'I can't think of anything more boring. Playing the piano is fun, but not all the time. Oh, sorry, Nicolas,' she added, suddenly realising what she'd just said. 'I forgot for a moment. Still, I'll bet you enjoy yourself a lot more doing what you're doing now than thumping away on the keys for hours and hours every day. Which is what I'd have to do if I wanted to become a concert pianist. I know because Mrs Johnson said so. "If you want to make a career of the piano, Felicity,"' she pronounced in a perfect imitation of Mrs Johnson's somewhat haughty

voice, '"you have to practise, practise, practise."
Well I practised like mad for weeks for tonight's
performance and I can tell you I've had more
than enough of that piano for a while. I'm not
going to touch a key over the Christmas
holidays. Now, I really do have to go help the
others with the food and stuff, or they'd think
I'm slacking. Thank you again, Nicolas,' she
said as she gave him a peck on the cheek. 'Don't
go without saying goodbye.'

'A vet,' Nicolas muttered drily as he watched
Felicity hurry away to join her friends. What a
horrible waste of talent!

'She's animal mad, is our Felicity,' Bert piped
up. 'Not domestic animals so much. Wildlife.
She and Kirsty—who's her very best friend, the
one who did the hip-hop dance—they're always
hunting around in the bush looking for injured
animals and birds. Kirsty's folks have an acreage
just out of town.'

'I see,' Nicolas said politely. Though he didn't
at all. All he could see was that she was wasting
a musical talent that was beyond exceptional.

'To tell the truth, Mr Dupre,' Bert went on,
'Mother and I are glad Felicity wants to be a vet.
That way, even if she goes away to study for a

while after leaving school, she'll eventually come back to live in this area. She's all we have now that our son has gone. Greg was an only child, you see. We always hoped that he and Serina would have more kiddies, but that wasn't to be.'

'His having had the mumps as a young lad had something to do with that,' Franny added. 'He had some tests done when Serina didn't fall for a baby again and they said he had a low sperm count. So we're lucky to have one grandchild. We'd be totally lost without Felicity, wouldn't we, Bert? She brings us such joy. Do you remember the day she was born? She was amazing from the word go. Didn't look like a newborn. Why, she could have passed for three months old. And she was so beautiful. Nothing like Greg when he was born. He looked like a wizened-up monkey for weeks. Of course she's taken after Serina with her looks and her musical talent. Not so much in nature though. Felicity's a real little goer, as I'm sure you've gathered, but extremely stubborn. It's thankful she has a good heart to temper her ambitions. But I know Serina has trouble with her sometimes. We help as much as we can. And Serina's mother does, too, of course. The girl really needs a father figure.

Greg was wonderful with her, not too indulgent. He recognised she needed direction. Felicity adored him. Oh dear,' Franny said suddenly, her eyes suddenly filling with tears. 'Sorry. I thought I was over doing this.'

Somehow, Nicolas managed to murmur something sympathetic. But his mind was whirling with the things Felicity's grandmother had just told him.

If she was Felicity's grandmother, Nicolas began thinking with a sick, hollow feeling forming in the pit of his stomach... Surely Serina wouldn't have done that? Surely not? But the evidence he'd just heard suggested differently.

His eyes started to scan the room, searching for her.

'Come on, Mother,' Bert said gently as he took his weeping wife's arm. 'Let's go get you a nice cup of tea. Lovely talking to you, Mr Dupre. And thanks once again for donating that terrific sum of money. You've made Felicity one extremely happy girl tonight.'

Serina knew, the moment her eyes met Nicolas's across the crowded hall, that what she'd feared would happen ever since she heard Nicolas was returning to Rocky Creek had just happened.

Never had she seen Nicolas look at her like that. There wasn't just anger in his eyes, or disbelief... There was sheer unadulterated horror.

'God help me,' she muttered under her breath as he came striding towards her, where she was thankfully standing by herself behind the drinks table.

'We need to talk, Serina,' he growled. 'Now!'

'What about?' she asked with feigned innocence whilst her heart was thudding wildly behind her ribs and nausea swirled in her stomach.

His eyes narrowed on her, his expression uncompromising in the extreme. 'I think you know what about.'

'Not unless you tell me.'

'You really want me to say it here? To shout out to all and sundry that Felicity is not your husband's daughter, but mine,' he hissed. 'Because I will if you don't make some excuse and come with me right here and now.'

Serina thought she was going to faint as she saw her whole world crashing around her. Not just her world, but her daughter's as well. And lots of other people's.

But he can't know, came the saving thought as she gripped the edge of the table, steadying her body as well as her mind. *He just suspects. You can bluff this out, girl. You have to bluff it out.*

'I can't imagine what Franny and Bert said to you to make you think such an outrageous thing,' she said with superb calm. 'But you're dead wrong. Felicity is Greg's daughter. Not yours.' Which she was, in every way but biologically.

'I don't believe you, Serina,' he challenged. 'Now are we going to argue about this here, or are you going to come with me?'

'Come where?' Not his apartment. No way was she going to go there again!

'Somewhere private,' he spluttered.

Felicity's bouncing up to her mother right at that moment with Kirsty by her side was both a blessing and a curse.

'Kirsty wants me to go to her place for a sleep-over,' she said. 'Can I, Mum? Can I, please?'

'Felicity, I…'

'Oh, please, Mrs Harmon,' Kirsty begged. 'Mum says it's okay. Then we could spend tomorrow together.'

Serina knew there would be no dissuading them, not once they ganged up on her. On top of that, it provided her with the perfect solution over where to take Nicolas. She would feel much safer facing him in her own home; safer, and stronger.

'All right, then,' she said, relenting. 'What about clothes?'

'She can borrow some of mine, Mrs Harmon,' Kirsty said. 'We're exactly the same size.'

'Fine. Just don't go doing anything silly.'

'Like what?'

'Like going too far into the bush looking for more sick koalas. The weather forecast for tomorrow is very hot, even hotter than today, and windy—perfect bushfire weather. Promise me you'll stay close to Kirsty's place.'

'We promise,' the two girls chorused.

'You could go out with Nicolas again tonight, if you wanted to,' Felicity added, and Kirsty giggled.

It didn't surprise Serina that her daughter was still trying to matchmake her with Nicolas. That girl never let up, once she got a bee in her bonnet. If only she knew!

'What a good idea,' Nicolas said immediately with a coldly cryptic smile. 'I enjoyed the time I spent with your mother today very much. We've always been great mates. We could go the movies, Serina, like we used to.'

Serina felt all the blood drain from her face.

Because of course they never went to the movies in the past. They just told their parents that was where they were going. They always spent the time making love.

If he thought he could somehow coerce her into having more sex with him, then he was sadly mistaken. But then an appalling thought popped into her head. What if he said he'd tell everyone in Rocky Creek he was Felicity's father if she didn't do just that?

Surely he wouldn't do a wicked thing like that. Surely not!

Nicolas saw her moment of realisation. Saw, also, the way her chin rose, her eyes spearing his with tigerish fury.

'I'm way too tired to go to the movies,' she returned coolly. 'But you can come back to my place for some coffee, if you like.'

He didn't like. He didn't want to go where she'd played happy family with Greg Harmon with his daughter. But he could hardly make a fuss in front of Felicity and her friend.

Frankly, Nicolas wasn't sure what he was going to do as yet. Except make Serina suffer for a while.

She deserved to suffer, if what he suspected was true.

'An excellent idea,' he said crisply.

'I can't leave straight away,' Serina said once Felicity and Kirsty ran off together. 'I have to help clean up here. As you can see, the party's coming to a close and there's lots of mess. All the plastic chairs have to be stacked up and put away as well.'

Nicolas controlled himself with difficulty. He was used to getting his own way with things, used to people jumping to do his bidding.

Serina was clearly past doing his bidding. It came to him suddenly that she'd only appeared to do so this afternoon because she had a secret agenda. To get him out of Rocky Creek as soon as possible. As much as she might have seemed to enjoy his lovemaking, she was probably faking it, the same way she'd faked her mad passion that night at the Opera House. All to get him to have sex with her without protection. All to conceive the child that she knew Greg Harmon couldn't give her.

A dark fury—and even darker desires—filled his soul as he thought about that night. What a fool he'd been! A blind besotted fool! But he would have her again—tonight. And she'd let him. Because that would be his bargain. One more night of sex in exchange for his silence, plus his departure tomorrow…

CHAPTER SIXTEEN

SERINA expected him to argue with her. But he didn't.

'In that case, I'll help,' he said. 'That way, you'll be finished more quickly.'

Which was true. Nicolas, the celebrated entrepreneur, was also a splendid organiser. Within thirty minutes everything was cleared away, the floors swept, the chairs stacked. Fortunately, during this time, her mother had left to take a tired Mrs Johnson home and Felicity had gone off with Kirsty and her parents.

Night was just falling when they emerged from the hall at eight-thirty, by which time Serina had her arguments all fixed firmly in her mind. She clung to the fact that Nicolas had no proof, just suspicion.

'It's still very hot out here,' he complained straight away. 'I hope your place has air-conditioning. If it doesn't we'll be going elsewhere.'

Serina kept her temper with difficulty. 'It has air-conditioning. On a timer, which I set for eight. The house should be nice and cool by the time we get there. But even if it wasn't, I wouldn't be going anywhere else with you, Nicolas Dupre.'

'Is that so?' came his cold reply. 'That's a matter to be seen. My wheels are over here.' And he took a hold of her arm.

She would have wrenched her arm away if other people hadn't been nearby. 'I have my own wheels, thank you very much,' she said and extracted herself carefully from his grasp. 'It's the white car over there. You can follow me home, it's not far.'

'How far?'

'Less than a kilometre. I live up at the top end of Winter Street. Remember the old strawberry farm? Well, developers bought it, tore down the dump of a farmhouse and turned it into a very nice estate. Greg and I bought a block of land there not long after we got married.'

Nicolas really didn't want to hear about Serina's life with Greg Harmon. He was still finding it hard to believe what she'd done. The girl he'd known—and loved—wasn't capable of

such deception. There again, the girl who'd
come to him that night at the Opera House
hadn't been that same girl. She'd been engaged
to Greg Harmon by then. Madly in love with
him, obviously, and ready to do anything for
him.

But what she'd done had been downright
wicked!

If that was what she did, another voice piped
up in his head. One that wasn't quite so ready to
condemn. One that was still connected to reason.
*You might be wrong, Nicolas. Not about Felicity
being your daughter, but about how and why
she was conceived. Serina might not have
planned anything. Maybe it just...happened.*

*But if that was the case, then why did she go
through with marrying Harmon? Why didn't she
come to me? I would have married her. I loved her.*

No, he was right the first time. She'd planned
it all right.

He knew women could do such things. His
own mother had.

His heart hardened once again towards Serina.
She had to be made to tell him the truth. Okay,
so he probably wouldn't blackmail her back into
his bed. Even he could not condone that kind of

outrageous behaviour, much as his dark side relished the idea. That had just been his anger talking and a primal urge for vengeance.

By the time Serina pulled in to the driveway of a cream, cement-rendered, ranch-style home, Nicolas had himself come halfway to reason. But only halfway. He wasn't in the mood for any bulldust from her.

'I hope you're not going to keep on denying it,' were his first words on joining her on the neat front porch.

She ignored him and went on unlocking the front door.

'Watch your feet,' she finally said when she pushed the door open. 'I have a cat who just loves to wind herself around your legs. Her name is Midnight.'

Nicolas wasn't one for pets, but he didn't mind cats. He quite liked their independence.

Not that Serina's cat seemed to be displaying much of that. She almost tripped both of them up in her rush for attention. Serina eventually scooped the big black cat up into her arms and carried her down the cream-tiled hallway into an open-planned living area that combined the kitchen, dining and sitting rooms.

'Yes, yes,' she said soothingly, stroking the cat's glossy black fur for a while before dropping her onto the kitchen floor. 'Mummy's home. I suppose you're hungry.' And she turned away to open the refrigerator door.

Nicolas could see that any hope of conversation was nil till the cat was attended to. So he sat down on one of the cane stools that fronted the breakfast bar and shut his mouth whilst he watched Serina fix her pet's food.

Eventually, however, his eyes strayed to his immediate surroundings.

For a house that hadn't looked all that large from the street, the inside was extremely spacious, especially this section where there was enough room for a couple of loungers, a huge television, lots of side tables and a large, oval-shaped dining table that would easily seat ten people. The floor was tiled in the same cream tiles as the hallway, but with well-placed rugs for warmth and comfort. The walls were cream, the furniture in various shades of brown and green. It was a well-designed area, perfect for family living and gatherings.

Before he could stop himself, Nicolas began thinking of all the family get-togethers that would have taken place in this room: the birthdays parties, the anniversaries, the Christmases.

He stared at Serina and wondered if she'd ever felt guilty over what she'd done. It seemed impossible that she hadn't given him a second thought over the years. He was her daughter's father, for pity's sake.

There again, this whole situation seemed impossible.

Suddenly, her fussing over Midnight annoyed the hell out of him.

'If you've finally finished with that damned animal,' he snapped, 'do you think we might get back to the subject at hand?'

She stood up and glared at him, her shoulders as straight as her gaze. 'Look, I already told you. Felicity is Greg's daughter, not yours. I can't imagine what Bert and Franny told you to make you believe otherwise.'

'Several things,' he shot back at her. 'Firstly, they expressed their gratitude that their son had been lucky enough to have at least one child. It seems having mumps as an adolescent can lead to sterility.'

'Greg was not sterile,' she countered quite firmly, 'and I can prove it. We had tests done when we didn't conceive another child. He did have a low sperm count. But he could still have become a father.'

'But not of a musical prodigy,' Nicolas snapped. 'Serina, do you think I'm totally blind? How many twelve-year-old girls can play like Felicity did tonight? She didn't come from some tone-deaf father!'

'She's my daughter, too, you know,' Serina argued, her face becoming quite flushed. 'I wasn't half-bad at music.'

'You were merely adequate.'

Her hands found her hips. 'Oh, thank you very much.'

'You can snap and snarl all you like. But I know what I know. Felicity is my daughter.'

'In that case, how can you explain her birth date, which can also be verified? Felicity was born exactly nine months after our wedding day, ten months after I slept with you that night. Since you're such a genius, you should be able to do the maths. She couldn't possibly be your daughter!'

Nicolas had been waiting for this argument to surface.

'I fell for that argument once before, Serina,' he retorted, finding calm in the face of her growing hysteria. 'But not tonight. Bert and Franny also waxed lyrical about how beautiful Felicity looked when she was born. Nothing like their son, who'd been all wrinkly. Not like a newborn at all, Franny said.'

He watched as Serina struggled to find something to say. But failed.

'She was late being born, wasn't she?' he charged. 'Very late.'

'Don't be ridiculous!' she spluttered. 'No doctor worth his salt would let a mother go that late these days. He would have given me an induction.'

'The doctor probably didn't know you were that late. Because you gave him the wrong dates. Now let me guess. You didn't have an ultrasound during your pregnancy. You made up some excuse about being superstitious about them. Maybe I could ask your mother and verify my suspicions.'

Serina crossed her arms. 'What you're saying is just so much rubbish! I don't know if you're mad, or just delusional.'

'If you keep denying it, Serina, I will have a DNA test done and then there will be no further arguments.'

Her arms fell open, as did her mouth. 'You can't do that! Not without my permission.'

'Oh, yes I can. Trust me. All I need is a good lawyer and a court order. Soon, I'll have what you've denied me for twelve years. Proof of my paternity, then access to my daughter.'

'Don't do this, Nicolas!' Serina cried, coming forward to grip the edge of the countertop.

'Don't do what?'

'Don't destroy your daughter's life.'

'So she is my daughter.'

There was a stricken silence from Serina, then a long shuddering sigh as her head drooped. 'Yes,' she confessed brokenly. 'Yes, she's your daughter!'

Nicolas felt like someone had struck him. It was one thing to suspect something, quite another to hear it from the only person who knew. He was sitting there, stunned, when her head lifted, her eyes flooded with tears.

'I'm sorry, Nicolas,' she choked out, 'so sorry.'

'She's sorry,' he repeated numbly.

'I never meant to hurt you. I never meant any of it. What I did…it was wrong. But not intentional.'

'Not intentional,' he repeated, all the while trying to control the emotions welling up inside him. Not fury so much anymore. In its place was a deep sadness, and a dreadful, dreadful emptiness.

'By the time I found out I was pregnant,' she cried, 'the wedding was upon me and I…I didn't have the courage to just walk away.'

'You should have told me,' he said bleakly.

'I should have. Yes.'

'But you didn't.'

'No.'

'You didn't love me. You loved him.'

Again, she fell silent, shaking her head from side to side.

'Did you know Harmon couldn't have kids when you slept with me? Did you do it to give him the child you knew he couldn't have.'

Nicolas could not deny the shock that filled her face. 'No! No! I would never do a thing like that. And Greg could have children. I told you. He just had a low sperm count.'

'If that's the case, when did you know she was mine?'

'Oh, God,' she sobbed, then snatched a handful of tissues from a box on the counter, turning away from him as she blew her nose.

'I'm waiting for an answer, Serina,' Nicolas said with barely held patience.

Her sigh was weary, her eyes haunted. 'I knew all along,' she confessed. 'I…I hadn't slept with

Greg during the last couple of months of our engagement. He wanted to make our wedding night special, he said.'

'And was it?' Nicolas asked bitterly.

'I'm not going to answer that.'

'You'll answer anything I ask you. And you'll do anything I ask you. Or you know what will happen. I'll tell everyone in Rocky Creek the truth and to hell with you.'

'You wouldn't do that. You're not that cruel.'

'How do you know? Like you said earlier today, we don't know each other anymore.'

'What is it that you want me to do?' she asked him, her eyes fearful.

'That depends on what you want me to do. Spell it out for me, Serina. That way I won't be under any further illusions about you.'

'I…I don't want you to tell anyone. Ever. I want you to keep my secret. Not for my sake. For Felicity's. And for her extended family. You must have seen how much Greg's parents love her. It would break their hearts—and Felicity's—if you tell them Greg wasn't her father.'

'And what about my heart? Or don't you think it can be broken?'

'Oh, Nicolas, Nicolas, do be honest. It's only your ego that is hurt by this. You don't have any bond with Felicity. It's not as though you want to come back to Rocky Creek and be her father for real. You hate it here. Your life is in New York and London.'

Amazing how the ugly truth could rub one raw. Though it was going a bit far to say that only his ego was hurting.

'She could come with me,' he said stubbornly. 'I could help her become a truly great pianist. She has the talent.'

Serina pulled a face. 'You don't know your daughter even a little bit if you say that. She doesn't want to be a concert pianist. She wants to be a vet.'

'Yes, I know,' he said grimly. 'She told me.'

'See? There's nothing to be gained by telling her that you're her father. She would end up hating you for it, believe me.'

'And you, Serina? Would you end up hating me? Or do you already hate me?'

Her eyes carried extreme frustration. 'I never hated you, Nicolas. But I could, quite easily, if you do this.'

'Are you talking about my telling everyone

Felicity is my daughter? Or what sexual favours I might demand in exchange for my silence?'

'Oh, Nicolas, Nicolas,' she said, her soulful eyes chastening, then infuriating him.

'It's not too much to ask, surely,' he bellowed at her. 'One miserable night for a future lifetime of silence? You might even enjoy it. You seemed to this afternoon.'

She went very pale. But her chin went up and she eyed him with the same strength of character with which she'd eyed him all day.

'This afternoon was something else entirely.'

'Really? You mean you didn't agree to do whatever I wanted in bed in exchange for my rapid departure tomorrow?'

'I know it probably looks that way…'

'I can't see how it can look any other way. So, if I asked you for a repeat performance tonight, you'd agree?'

She just stared at him, her eyes reproachful.

'If I must,' she said at last.

Her answer took all the breath from his lungs. And struck a vicious blow to his conscience.

It came to Nicolas then just how much Serina loved their daughter. It was a love that transcended pride; that would endure any humiliation to protect her child from harm, or unhappiness.

His own mother had loved him that way.

His father, however, had not given a damn about him. Nicolas had caught up with him a few years ago and told him he was his son. The man had not only denied it, but he'd also spoken disparagingly about his mother, inferring she was some kind of sleep-around slut, which Nicolas knew wasn't true. Nicolas hadn't expected his father to love him. But he could have been kind, not cruel. Could have been decent.

He had the chance to be kind now…to be decent.

'It's all right, Serina,' he said with a weary sigh of his own. 'I won't ask that of you. You win. I'll walk away. And I won't say a word about being Felicity's father.'

She immediately burst into floods of tears.

'Don't cry,' he snapped. 'I'm not doing it for you. But for her. For my daughter.'

Serina lifted her head from her hands, her wet eyes beseeching. 'You just don't understand anything, do you? I loved you, Nicolas. I loved you so much. I thought you loved me, but you didn't. You left me when I needed you. And you never came back. I couldn't forgive you for that. But I couldn't forget you, either.'

They stared at each other for a long time.

Nicolas was the first to speak.

'Did you love Harmon as much as you loved me?'

'I learned to love him,' she said. 'He was a good man. But my heart has always been yours, Nicolas. You were my first love, my first and only grand passion.'

As she was his.

'Spend the night with me,' he said, his voice breaking a little.

Her eyes showed total disbelief.

'I won't put any conditions on your doing so. I promise I won't say anything to anyone about Felicity whether you say yes or no. Please, Serina, I just want…' He broke off before he broke down.

'What, Nicolas?' she asked with a tortured groan. 'What is it that you want?'

'Just you. In my arms. One more time.'

'You don't know what you're asking,' she choked out. 'If I do this, I'll fall hopelessly in love with you again and I won't want you to go. I've never been able to resist you in bed, Nicolas. You must know that by now.'

'It is some small comfort,' he returned. 'So what's it to be, my love? Yes, or no?'

'Oh…' She shook her head from side to side before lancing him with a despairing look. 'Not here,' she blurted out.

Nicolas took that as a yes. So did his body.

'I'll follow you back to your place in Port,' she said, her eyes already glittering brightly. 'But I won't be staying the whole night.'

Nicolas nodded….

CHAPTER SEVENTEEN

WHEN Serina woke, a pre-dawn light was filtering through the window above the bed head.

So much for my resolve not to stay the whole night, she thought ruefully as she glanced at her wristwatch and saw that it was five past six. Sighing, she very carefully lifted her leg off Nicolas's still-sleeping form and rolled onto her back next to him.

She'd been right to be fearful of staying the night with him. Nicolas in passionate mode was difficult enough to resist; Nicolas, the tender lover, was impossible to resist.

She hadn't fallen hopelessly in love with him again. How could she when she was already in love with him? But she'd begun to have foolish hopes where he was concerned, very foolish hopes, indeed.

Down deep, she knew that he wasn't going to

come back to Rocky Creek to live. Neither was he going to marry her. The most Serina could hope was that he'd stay for the week that he'd booked. And perhaps come back for the odd visit over the coming years.

But more than likely he was going to get on that plane today and never return.

Last night had had goodbye written all over it.

Her heart turned over at this last thought. How was she going to be able to stand losing him again?

You'll just have to, came the harsh voice of reason. *You have no other choice. Mothers can't afford to have mental breakdowns. Now get your butt moving, get dressed and go home before all the neighbours wake up and see you driving past still dressed in the clothes you were wearing last night.*

Such thinking propelled her out of bed like a shot. Her clothes, fortunately, weren't strewn all over the place as they had been yesterday afternoon. Nicolas had undressed her here, with care, in the bedroom. Scooping them up, she hurried into the bathroom, where she climbed into the shower. Five minutes later, she was out, dried and dressed.

That was another thing mothers learned to do: be quick.

Having rinsed her mouth out with cold water, she was finger-combing her hair into place when the bathroom door opened and there stood Nicolas in all his naked glory.

'And where do you think you're going at this hour?' he asked.

Serina thought her nonplussed expression was of Oscar-winning standards. 'Home, of course,' she said coolly.

'But why? Felicity's not there. And you don't go into the office on a Saturday.'

'I have to this morning,' she returned crisply. 'Emma's having the day off. She's going to a wedding.'

'You still don't have to go this early. It's only ten past six. Have coffee with me first. I have something I want to discuss with you.'

Her heart leapt, not with hope, but with fear. Surely he hadn't changed his mind about not disclosing the fact he was Felicity's biological father? 'What about?' she asked somewhat warily.

'Nothing for you to worry about. Look, I'll go put on the kettle,' he said, and turned away, giving her a perfect view of his perfect rear.

'Only if you put some clothes on first?' she called after him.

He just laughed.

By the time she dared to leave the bathroom and join him in the living area he'd pulled on a pair of black satin boxer shorts.

'So what is it you want to talk to me about?' she asked whilst he opened a couple of the coffee bags supplied and popped them into mugs.

'I've been thinking,' he replied slowly, then stopped to pour in the boiling water.

'About what?'

'You take milk and one sugar, don't you?'

'Yes,' she said grudgingly. 'Now what's all this about?'

'My, my, but you are not such a happy chappy in the mornings, are you?' he said as he proceeded to take his time, getting the milk out of the fridge then slowly opening a packet of sugar.

'Nicolas, you're driving me mad! I have to get going. The neighbours will wake up soon and they'll see me coming home still dressed in this.' And she indicated the white dress she'd worn the night before.

His eyebrows lifted. 'Oh, I see. I forgot that

people noticed such things in Rocky Creek. Not only noticed, but cared. Now don't blow a gasket,' he added when he saw a dark frustration fill her face. 'This won't take long. The thing is, Serina, I've changed my mind.'

Oh, no, she thought in a panic.

'It's not what you're thinking.' He frowned suddenly. 'Why must you always think the worst? What I've changed my mind about is leaving today.'

'But last night, you said...' She broke off, not sure if she was happy now with his change of heart. Amazing how things could work out in your head when they were romantic fantasies. Everything became much more complicated in real life.

'I know what I said. But I've had more time to think things through and there's no reason for me to leave today. Look, I'm not going to say anything about being Felicity's father. I gave you my word on that. I can see how cruel that would be, and pointless. Felicity would probably hate me, as you said. And you, too. Which is not what I want. Not at all,' Nicolas added, then came forward to draw her into his arms. 'You said there was a danger you'd fall hopelessly in love with me again last night. Dare I hope it might have happened? Or is that just wishful thinking on my part?'

Serina groaned as her heart began to battle with her head. To tell him that she loved him was a big step and, perhaps, a foolish one at this juncture. After all, he hadn't said he loved her and he'd had plenty of chances last night.

'Nicolas, I can't afford to have my heart broken by you again,' she said carefully.

'You think I would do that?'

'I don't know what you'd do. Like you said, we don't know each other anymore. On top of that, we come from different worlds.'

'That's not quite true. We're both Australians. If you'd ever spent time living overseas, you'd realise that Australians are a breed apart. Look, I appreciate that you think I hate it here in Rocky Creek and that I prefer living in New York, et cetera, et cetera et cetera,' he said as he pushed her coffee across the kitchen counter towards her. 'But do you know what? I'm not so sure I hate Rocky Creek as much as I thought I did. Frankly, I enjoyed yesterday's talent quest more than I've enjoyed anything in years. But all that pales into insignificance against what we have together. Do you honestly think I'm going to let you get away from me for a third time? Okay, so I probably wouldn't like to live here full-time,' he went on. 'But there's no reason why I can't visit on a regular basis. No reason why you can't visit me as well. I'll pay all your expenses, of course.'

Of course, Serina thought, an unexpectedly sour taste filling her mouth. That was what wealthy men did for their mistresses: they paid.

Becoming Nicolas's part-time, long-distance mistress was not the stuff Serina's romantic dreams were made of. Especially since he hadn't even said he loved her. On top of that, to have him visit her in Rocky Creek on a regular basis was still a risk.

Her face twisted with the reality of that risk. 'You promise you won't say anything about you-know-what? Not ever? Even if you get angry with me for some reason?'

'I give you my solemn word.'

'So what, exactly, am I to tell my family? Especially my mother. She's going to ask questions if you stick around for another week.'

'Tell her the truth. That I've fallen hopelessly in love with you again and can't bring myself to leave just yet.'

Serina's mouth fell open. It was still open when Nicolas kissed her.

Nicolas leant over the railing of the balcony, calling and waving to Serina as she crossed the road to where she'd parked her car. When she glanced up and threw him a kiss, he threw one back.

'I'll ring you later,' he shouted, and she smiled.

It made him feel good, that smile. She made him feel good.

Okay, so she didn't quite trust him enough to tell him that she loved him, too. But he'd felt her love last night, and in her kisses just now. Soon, she would say the words he wanted to hear. Meanwhile, he'd begin making concrete plans for their future together, sensible ones that he could live with on a permanent basis.

There was no doubt in Nicolas's mind that existing 24/7 in Rocky Creek was beyond him. He would eventually miss the things which had become an integral part of his life. Going to stimulating dinner parties, the theatre, the opera. Serina was right about that.

But one didn't have to go to London or New York for such cultural diversions.

There were plenty of cities in Australia that could cater to his occasional need for such activities. Sydney especially, which was only a short flight from Port Macquarie. It might take some time, but he would sell his apartments in London and New York and buy a place in Sydney, as well as one in Port Macquarie. He would inquire if there was an apartment for sale in this building, he thought as he walked back inside and set about making himself a fresh cup of coffee. That way he could commute between both places with ease, and without feeling like he had no home. He could even continue his career as a producer and promoter, if he felt so inclined. Just because he hadn't brought shows to Australia in the past didn't mean he couldn't in future. Sydney had several theatres large enough to hold even the most lavish musicals. And the Opera House administrators were always trying to persuade the world's top singers and musicians to come Down Under.

Admittedly, he'd been growing a bit bored with that part of his life lately, but Nicolas was old enough to know that he might grow unbored at some future date. Showbiz was in his blood. To suddenly drop it from his life would be a recipe for disaster. He'd seen many a marriage flounder because of one or either party thinking their spouse would change after the wedding.

And he meant to marry Serina.

He hadn't mentioned the M-word yet—fearing it was a little premature—but she wasn't going to get away from him this time.

He'd done a lot of thinking overnight. He still loved her. And he'd finally come to the sensible realisation that he was crazy to feel any jealousy over her life with Greg Harmon. Her marrying another man was entirely his fault. If he'd been there for her in the first place, if he'd shown her by his actions that he truly loved her, instead of letting his stupid male pride ruin everything, then she would never have married Harmon. Her statement that she'd learned to love her husband had been very telling. She'd never been in love with Harmon the way she had with him.

He could spend the rest of his life tormenting himself over what might have been. But what would be the point of that? If nothing else, Nicolas was not the kind of man to cry over spilt milk. When things got tough, he got even tougher.

With his fresh coffee finally made, he carried it back out onto the balcony where the morning sunshine wasn't yet too fierce, just pleasantly warm. It was, after all, only six-thirty in the morning. But the day promised to be a sizzler: high thirties, someone had said last night.

Now that was one thing he'd have to get used to again: the long hot summers.

Thank heavens for air-conditioning and cool balconies that faced the sea….

CHAPTER EIGHTEEN

'WELL, well, well,' Allie said with a knowing smile when Serina walked into the office shortly after nine. 'We didn't expect to see you in here this morning. We thought you'd be home in bed, catching up on the sleep you didn't get last night.'

Serina tried not to look either guilty or surprised. 'Don't tell me,' she said drily as she walked past a grinning Allie. 'The Rocky Creek grapevine has been at it already.' She'd thought she'd managed to sneak back home without her neighbours seeing. Obviously that hadn't been the case.

'No need to get defensive, love,' her mother piped up from where she was sitting at Emma's desk. 'Everyone's pleased as punch that you've finally decided to get out and enjoy yourself a bit. Did you have a nice time?'

Serina wasn't sure what to make of her mother's attitude. She would have expected more disapproval. She decided to play it cool and see what happened. There was no way she could follow Nicolas's advice and just blurt out that they were madly in love. Her mother, for one, would think she was crazy!

'Very nice, thank you,' she said as she crossed the room to her own desk. 'We went to a club for a while and I'm afraid I had too much to drink. So Nicolas let me bunk down on his sofa till I sobered up. Next thing I knew the sun was coming up.' Serina suspected this story just might be believed. She had a reputation for being stand-offish with men, so it would seem unlikely that she'd jump into bed with Nicolas so quickly.

'I suppose he's staying in a pretty snazzy place,' her mother said. 'A man like him.'

Serina dropped her bag on a nearby filing cabinet before pulling out her office chair. 'I thought I told you the other night. He's rented an apartment in the new Blue Horizons building.' She sat down and turned on her computer. 'Maybe I didn't.' She'd been very distracted during that phone call. Spending the afternoon in bed with Nicolas did that to her. 'Yes, it's a very snazzy place with a lovely view. He's decided to stay on there for another week.'

'Another week! But he told Mrs Johnson and me just last night that he was leaving today.'

'He was going to. But he's changed his mind and extended his booking. Since he'll still be in Port for Christmas, Mum, I...er...thought I'd ask him to join us on Christmas Day.'

'Are you sure that's a good idea? I mean... Christmas Day is for family.'

Serina's heart turned over. If only her mother knew. Nicolas was family. He was her grand-daughter's father. 'Family and friends, Mum,' she said firmly. 'I'm sure Franny and Bert won't mind. And Felicity will be delighted. She likes Nicolas a lot, you know.'

'Yes, I know. She never stops talking about him.'

'Then there's no problem, is there?'

'I guess not,' her mother said. Suddenly, she didn't look so approving, confirming Serina's suspicion that any relationship she had with Nicolas might be frowned upon. She could not imagine her mother being pleased with her daughter becoming any man's mistress.

'Can I come for Christmas, too?' Allie piped up with a mischievous grin.

Serina smiled. 'I don't think your parents would be too pleased with that idea.'

'Darn. Oops. Incoming call. Browns Landscaping and Building Supplies,' she trilled. 'Oh, Mr Dupre! We were just talking about you. Yes, yes, all right…Nicolas… Yes, she does that sometimes. Just a sec. Serina,' Allie called out. 'Nicolas said you've got your cell phone turned off and could you please turn it back on.'

Serina tried not to look flustered as she stood up and retrieved her phone from her bag. There she'd been, handling everything quite well, she thought, then bingo, Nicolas called and she was immediately in a state. In a way, she wished he hadn't told her that he loved her this morning. It could make her go crazy, if she let it. Crazy with wanting and hoping and…and just plain crazy!

'Tell him it's turned on now,' she said a little stiffly.

'It's turned on now, Nicolas. 'By-ee,' Allie finished, her voice having gone all soft and simpering.

Serina suppressed a sigh.

Ten seconds later, her vibrating mobile phone was dancing over the desktop. Serina snatched it up to her ear, telling herself all the while to stay cool. Her mother was listening and so was Allie. She had to be careful not to say anything that would contradict what she'd told them about last night.

'Hello, Nicolas,' she said. 'Sorry about the phone. It's a habit of mine. So what's up?'

There was a short sharp silence at the other end of the line, then Nicolas laughed. 'I get it. Your mum's there, isn't she?'

'Yep.'

'And you haven't told her about us.'

'Not exactly.'

'You bad girl, I'm going to have to take you in hand.'

'Yes, please.'

'Ooh, you are a bad girl. So when can I take you in hand? This afternoon too soon?'

'I'll have to see what Felicity is doing first. I'll give her a call and then get back to you.'

'Don't make me wait too long. I'm not a patient man. Not when I want something.'

Serina almost opened her drying mouth to ask him what he wanted. Fortunately, common sense won and she remained silent.

He laughed again, softly, sexily. 'You can't talk. I get it. Shall I tell you what I want in minute detail, with accompanying sound effects?'

'Not right now, Nicolas.'

'Oh, I love that schoolmarm voice you have at times.'

'I'll call you back after I've contacted Felicity, all right?'

He sighed. 'Spoilsport.'

Serina finally began to find some amusement in the situation.

'Yes, I know it's terribly hot,' she said. 'Why don't you go have a swim and cool down? 'Bye now. I'll call back soon.'

She hung up, but her mind was already on the time when she could be with Nicolas again, when he could take her in hand.

'Serina…'

Serina blinked, then turned her head towards her mother.

'You were going to call Felicity,' her mother reminded her.

'What? Oh, yes. I forgot for a moment.'

'I can see that….'

Serina resented the note of disapproval in her mother's voice. Heavens, it wasn't as though she was a neglectful mother.

Felicity answered straight away.

'Hi, Mum. How's things? You have a good time last night?'

'A great time,' Serina admitted. 'And you? I suppose you and Kirsty stayed up all night.' Sleepovers between girlfriends never involved much sleep.

'We passed out on the lounge around two, didn't we, Kirsty?'

'So what time do you want me to pick you up today?' Serina asked, knowing full well that it wouldn't be anytime soon. When those two got together, wild horses couldn't drag them apart.

'Not till dark,' Kirsty replied straight away. 'How about eight o'clock?'

'I don't like driving along that road in the dark.' Kirsty's place was a few kilometres out of town along a narrow winding road that had no lighting whatsoever. 'Could we make it seven?'

Serina heard some fierce negotiations going on in the background. 'Look, Kirsty's mum said I could stay for another night, if that's all right with you.'

'Are you sure? I think I should talk to her.'

Janine, Kirsty's mother, came on the phone

and it was finally agreed that Felicity could stay another night.

'How's the weather out your way?' Serina asked.

'Very hot,' Janine said. 'And windy.'

'Don't let the girls go too far into the bush, okay?'

Kirsty's place was on the edge of a state forest that was simply huge and very thick.

'Will do. Oh, and Serina?'

'Yes?'

'I thought you looked really lovely last night.'

'Why thank you. What a nice thing to say!'

'A little bird told me you went out with Nicolas Dupre after the party?'

'My, my, that little bird flies fast.'

Janine laughed. 'That's Rocky Creek for you. So is it true?'

'Yes.'

'And is it also true that he's an old flame of yours?'

Kirsty's family only moved into the area a few years ago, so they knew nothing of the time when Nicolas Dupre and Serina had been teenagers. Serina decided that she was tired of denying that they had some kind of relationship in the past. But she wasn't about to admit too much.

'Yes, he was,' she said.

'Lucky you. Do you think anything will come of it this time? I mean, is he sticking around or is this just a whirlwind visit?'

'I'm not sure yet, Janine.'

Which just about said it all. She wasn't sure. About anything.

The adrenalin rush that she'd felt earlier when Nicolas called had totally dissipated by the time she hung up. Was she being a fool, thinking they could make a lasting relationship this time?

'Serina…'

Serina blinked then turned to face her mother.

'What?'

'Could you come outside for a minute? I want to speak to you about something. Privately,' she added softly with a surreptitious glance Allie's way.

The heat hit them both the moment they stepped outside the door.

'Better make this quick, Mum,' Serina said as she moved back into the shade of the building's eaves. 'Or we're going to melt away.'

'I'm not sure I can be quick. To be honest, I'm not sure where to even start.'

Serina was taken aback before the penny

dropped. Her mother wanted to say something to her about last night but didn't have the courage. She'd never been one of those mothers to voluntarily bring up the subject of sex. If it had been left up to Margaret Brown, then Serina would never have learned the facts of life. She grew up, grateful that she lived in the country, and had been able to work things out for herself. Her father had been of a similar ilk, a shy man who wasn't given to conversations or confidences about private matters. Serina wasn't surprised that she was an only child.

'I'm beginning to get worried about you and Nicolas,' her mother blurted out at last.

'In what way?'

Her mother's face twisted into a mask of concern. 'I'm worried he's going to break your heart again. And don't go telling me that he didn't break your heart all those years ago. You can lie to Felicity if you want to. I wouldn't expect you to tell your daughter the truth.'

Serina's heart skipped a beat. 'The truth?'

'About you and Nicolas in the old days. I knew you were way more than just good friends. I knew you were sleeping together, right from the first night you went out with him. It was there, in your eyes, the next morning. You looked…different. Older.'

'Mum, I…'

'Oh, it's perfectly all right,' her mother interrupted. 'I'm not judging you. I never judged you. I understood exactly what you felt for that boy.'

'You did?'

'I felt the same way about a boy when I was around the same age. I was simply mad about him. Couldn't keep my hands off him.'

'Goodness!'

'There was nothing good about him, I can tell you. He was a wicked lad and he broke my heart. I was never the same after he dumped me. I couldn't bear for another boy to touch me for years. And then I met your father.' Tears filled her eyes. 'If it wasn't for your father I would never have gotten married, or had you. His tenderness was my saving grace. Plus his shyness. He was nothing like Hank. For which I was eternally grateful.'

'What… What happened to this Hank?'

'Got killed on his motorcycle when he was twenty-one. I still cried when he died. But I think it was more for my own sorry self than for him.'

'Oh, Mum. I had no idea.'

'How could you? I never told you. I've never talked to you at all much about myself, or even about you. When Nicolas left Rocky Creek I knew you were heart-broken. But I was afraid to talk to you. Afraid you might tell me what you'd been doing together. Afraid I might tell you what I went through. And I didn't want you to know. I didn't want you to be ashamed of me.'

'Ashamed of you! Why would I be ashamed of you?'

She flushed a beetroot red. 'The things I did with Hank. They were wicked.'

'Were they really, Mum? You loved him, didn't you?'

'More than I thought was ever possible.'

'There, you see?' She put her arms around her mother's shoulders and held her close. 'Not wicked at all. Just in love. Like Nicolas and I were. Like we still are.'

Her mother lifted wet eyes to Serina's. 'He loves you? He said that?'

'Just this morning, before he kissed me goodbye.'

'And he's going to stay this time?'

'Only for the next week. But he's promised to visit often.'

'Do you think you might get married one day?'

'No, Mum. I don't think that's ever going to happen.'

'You're a very brave girl, Serina, very brave and very strong. Did I ever tell you that?'

She had, actually. At Greg's funeral. But Serina thought it wasn't quite the right moment to mention that. Instead, she steered her mother back inside, where she made her a cup of tea, after which she surreptitiously carried her mobile phone into the ladies' and called Nicolas back.

'I thought you were never going to call,' he said sharply. 'I was getting worried.'

'No need. Everything's fine. Felicity's going to stay another night at Kirsty's. And I'm going to ask my mother to hold the fort for the rest of the day so that I can spend it with you.'

'Wow! They say all good things come to those who wait, but I've never believed it till now.'

'Oh, and there's one more thing.'

'What?'

'I love you….'

CHAPTER NINETEEN

NICOLAS had experienced several moments of happiness in his life.

But this moment surpassed all others: it was true happiness. He was stunned to feel tears pricking at his eyes. Never in all his forty years had he cried with happiness.

'Well you've done it now,' he choked out.

'What do you mean?'

'I'm never going to let you go now, Serina. Not if you love me.'

'I still won't go overseas with you, Nicolas. Well, I would…briefly. Just not permanently.'

'Even that small compromise shows me you do really love me.'

'You doubted me?'

'Might I remind you that you were the one who said I was only good for one thing.'

'Oh, Nicolas…I'm so sorry I said that. That wasn't nice. But you only have yourself to

blame. A girl tends to forget a man's other qual-
ities when one stands out.'

'You should be grateful that it stands out at all.
When a man approaches forty…'

She laughed. It was a delightful laugh.

'When can you get away?' he asked.

'Soon.'

'How soon?'

'Very soon,' she said softly.

An hour later, Nicolas was pacing the
pavement outside Blue Horizons, impatiently
waiting for Serina's car to arrive. The temperature had risen dramatically during the last sixty
minutes and a hot wind was whipping down the
street. He'd finally dressed sensibly in shorts and
T-shirt but was still feeling uncomfortably warm.

Suddenly, there she was, pulling up to the curb
opposite. Nicolas raced over and wrenched the
driver's door open.

'Why has it taken you so long?' he demanded
to know. 'I could have flown back to Sydney in
that time.'

She smiled up at him as she climbed out of the
car, looking cool and pretty in cream Bermuda
shorts and a lemon blouse.

'I was held up for a while with a builder who

wasn't happy with the timber we'd delivered to him. Sorry, but Mum isn't at her best dealing with difficult customers, and Allie's useless.'

Nicolas wasn't in the mood to be mollified. 'I thought you'd had an accident. You could have called me. That's what mobile phones are for.'

'I said I was sorry.' Her smile widened. 'My, but you're not a happy chappy when you have to wait for something,' she said, echoing his words of that morning. 'Now why don't you just kiss me and stop being obsessive compulsive?'

'Takes one to know one, sweetheart,' he growled, and pulled her into his arms. His kiss was deep and long and brought several toots from horns of passing motorists.

'I have something I want to show you,' he said when he finally came up for air.

'Not down here, I hope,' she teased. 'I don't want to be arrested for indecent exposure.'

'Very funny. No, it's nothing like that. I want you to come upstairs with me.'

She laughed. 'I already gathered that.'

Nicolas gave her a droll look. 'Will you get your mind off sex for the moment?'

'You mean you want to actually do something else?'

'No, I don't want to do something else. I just thought it might be wise to show you that I can do something else.'

'Such as what?'

'If you'll just be quiet for a minute or two,' he said as he steered her across the road, 'I'll show you.'

'I'm already speechless.'

Serina laughed when he ground to a halt and speared her with a fierce narrowed-eyed glance. 'You will be punished later for your sarcasm!'

'Oooh. Is that a promise or a threat?'

'Another twenty lashes for Madame!'

'Are we on the *Bounty* here, or in one of those old war films? You keep changing characters.'

'I am the master of disguise.'

'Good grief,' she said, laughing. 'It's Boris Karloff!'

'I'm not that old!'

'You're nearly forty.'

He pretended to look horrified. 'You must not mention the dreaded F word. Not unless you want to be punished.'

'That depends on the punishment.'

'You will be tied naked to my bed for the rest of the day.'

Her face fell in mock disappointment. 'Oh…is that all?'

'I will rub your entire body with oil.'

Her eyebrows arched coquettishly. 'What kind of oil?'

'What other kind is there?' he countered, flexing his biceps like Popeye. 'Olive oil!'

'You'll ruin the sheets.'

He waved nonchalantly. 'There are plenty more sheets where they came from. But first, we must ride up to the penthouse.'

'The penthouse! You've moved apartments?'

'Not as yet. But I'm thinking of buying the penthouse. It's for sale.'

'Oh, my!' Serina exclaimed as soon as she walked inside. 'This place is out of this world. But it must be worth a small fortune.'

'It's on the market for three-point-five million. But in this current economic climate, I think I can close the deal for three.'

'Far be it for me to persuade you otherwise, Nicolas,' Serina said as she wandered from the extensive and expensively furnished living area into the equally lavish master bedroom. 'But can you afford it?'

'My apartment in New York is worth five times

that much. I also own a town house in London worth at last two and a half mil. Pounds, that is. Neither have mortgages. So yes, I can afford it.'

She just stared at him. 'I didn't know you were that rich.'

He shrugged. 'I've been very fortunate. And very astute, when it comes to investments. I know there's a line in the show *The Producers* that says to never put your money in the show. But if you put your money in the right show, then the sky's the limit when it comes to profits. I've put my money into two super successful musicals. And I manage some extremely successful musicians. So yes, I'm very rich.'

And very used to getting his own way, Serina appreciated. It had to be very corrupting to be that rich, to be able to buy whatever you wanted.

Does he really love me? Serina suddenly worried as she gazed at the king-sized bed. *Or does he just want me?*

His hands curling over her shoulders startled her. She hadn't seen him move behind her.

'So what do you think, my darling?' he murmured as his lips brushed over her hair. 'Should I buy it, or not?'

Serina swallowed when he pulled her back

against him and she felt his hardness. 'It seems a lot of money for a place you'll hardly ever be in.'

'Oh, I don't know about that,' he said, taking his hands off her shoulders and moving them down under her arms and over the swell of her breasts. 'I have a feeling I'm going to be here quite a lot.'

Serina sucked in sharply when he started undoing the buttons on her blouse. 'What…what do you think you're doing?'

'What do you think I'm doing? You know I don't like making love with clothes on.'

'But we can't… Not here… Someone might come in…'

'Why would they? The girl on the desk said I could take all the time I wanted inspecting the place.'

'But someone still might come in…'

'I very much doubt it.'

Her blouse and bra were quickly disposed of.

'But they might,' she protested even as he unzipped her shorts.

'We'd hear them before they came in here. Ah. That's better,' he said as the shorts fell to the floor. 'Mmm. Very sexy panties but I prefer you without them.' Her underwear went the same way as the shorts, leaving her naked except for her sandals.

His right hand smoothed over her stomach, then dipped between her legs.

'Nicolas…please…I…I don't think I can relax.'

'I don't want you relaxed.'

She gasped when his other hand started playing with her extremely erect nipples.

'I want you as turned on as I am.'

When Serina moaned, he stopped what he was doing.

'Lie back across the bed,' he ordered her thickly. 'And touch yourself while I get naked.'

Why did she do it? Why?

Because she loved obeying him as much as she loved him. It was like a drug, the way he could make her feel.

'Yes, that's the way,' he said as he hurriedly stripped off his clothes. 'Open your legs a little wider, darling. You look so beautiful like that.'

Beautiful? More like brazen. For she no longer cared if anyone came in.

'Beautiful,' he said again as he knelt between her legs and lifted her hand away….

CHAPTER TWENTY

'SEE?' Nicolas said some considerable time later. 'Nobody came in.'

'Just as well,' she muttered.

'I'd like to get up and get dressed now,' she said, her willpower having returned.

'Are you sure you want to?'

'Nicolas! Get off me, please.'

'Oh, very well.' And he levered himself up off her body. 'Fancy a shower together?'

Serina winced. 'Haven't you had enough?'

'Of you? Never.'

'I wish you wouldn't say things like that.'

'Why?'

'Because it's unrealistic.' She scrambled to her feet and reached for her clothes. 'I need to go to the bathroom,' she snapped. 'Alone, if you don't mind.'

Nicolas frowned as he watched her go. She

still didn't trust him, he realised, didn't trust his love for her, or his commitment to her.

What could he do to reassure her? Ask her to marry him?

It seemed a premature move to Nicolas. But women saw things differently to men. An offer of marriage conjured up all sorts of romantic connotations for women. It spelt out love in ways that mere words couldn't.

Nicolas decided then and there to do just that. Tonight, over a candlelit dinner. He'd have to buy her an engagement ring first, of course, a really nice one. Port Macquarie was sure to have some decent jewellery shops. Tourist towns catered to people who had money and time on their hands to shop. It meant he would have to make some excuse to have a couple of hours alone this afternoon. He would say that he was tired and needed a nap before their night out. Sounded a bit lame but he couldn't think of anything else.

Meanwhile, he would have to get dressed, quick smart, so as not to annoy Serina further when she emerged from the bathroom. She hadn't been too pleased with his having his way with her a little while ago. But she only had herself to blame, kissing him the way she had when she arrived, then flirting with him so outrageously. Still, he would make sure that in future he kept their lovemaking to places where there was no possibility of their being disturbed.

He'd just pulled on his shirt when she opened the bathroom door, looking just a little wary. Till she saw he was properly dressed.

'I was thinking we might go for a drive around the beaches for the rest of this morning,' he said straight away. 'Then have a spot of lunch somewhere cool, overlooking the water.'

'Sounds good,' Serina said, feeling somewhat guilty for her attitude earlier. It wasn't as though he'd forced her to have sex. She'd been more than willing in the end.

'Great! But before we go, come and take a look at the view from the terrace. It goes for miles.'

It certainly did, from the horizon out to sea to the mountains in the west. The only minus at that moment was the heat and the westerly wind that whipped Serina's hair across her eyes as she tried to take in the full, 360-degree panorama.

'This would be superb on a warm winter's day,' she said as she struggled to hold her hair back. 'Or a balmy summer evening.'

'But not today,' Nicolas said. 'I agree. I just wanted you to see it. Let's get going.'

As Serina turned away from the glass security fence that surrounded the terrace, a whiff of smoke suddenly teased her nostrils. Frowning, she anchored her hair back from her face more securely and stared in the direction the wind was coming from.

West.

'Nicolas!' she said sharply. 'Come over here.'

He hurried to her side. 'What is it?'

'Over there,' she said, pointing towards the mountain range in the distance. 'Can you see it?'

'See what?'

'Smoke.'

Nicolas narrowed his eyes against the glare of the sunshine and peered hard in the direction of Serina's finger.

'Yes. I can see it,' he confirmed.

'Oh, my God! It's a bushfire, isn't it? Over Rocky Creek way.'

'There's no need to panic. From what I can see it's only small and probably in the state forest. The one beyond Rocky Creek. They used to have fires in there practically every summer, but they never reached the town.'

She turned to him, her eyes full of worry. 'But you don't understand. The town has spread. And the people Felicity's staying with this weekend, they live right on the edge of that state forest. With this wind, the fire won't be small for long and it could be upon them before you can say boo.'

'Surely the rural fire service would evacuate them, if there was any danger.'

'Like they did in Victoria?' she countered despairingly. 'Even if we had the resources, which we don't, things can go very wrong very quickly. In extreme weather conditions like this, sometimes there's not enough time to evacuate everyone. There are lots more people living out in the bush now than when you lived in Rocky Creek. Kirsty's parents live farther away than most. And there's only one access road. What kind of stupid mother am I to let Felicity stay there this weekend? I knew the weather forecast. And I know the dangers. Greg drummed them into me. If anything happens to Felicity…' she cried, her face going ashen at the thought.

Nicolas had faced several crises in his life but none had ever affected him the way this had. Serina claimed he had no real bond with Felicity.

That clearly wasn't true. The rush of love and protectiveness he felt for his daughter was very real indeed. As was his fear for her safety. But he had to keep a cool head. Nothing was to be gained by panicking.

'We can't be sure yet where the fire is, Serina. Or how close it might be to Felicity. But let's not dillydally. Let's go get your daughter.'

Serina lifted her big brown eyes to his.

'Our daughter,' she choked out.

Keeping a cool head suddenly became more difficult. Action came to Nicolas's rescue.

'We'll take the four-wheel drive,' he asserted. 'You can phone the people that Felicity's staying with on the way. Do you have their number?'

'It's in my menu. Yes.'

'Good.'

Her mobile didn't work till they were out of the basement car park and on the road.

'There's no answer,' she said, alarm in her voice.

'That might be good news, Serina. They might have made the sensible decision to get out early.'

'Then why didn't they put a message on their answering machine? And why didn't they call me? No, this doesn't feel right. Something's wrong. I'll try Felicity's mobile.'

It rang but there was no answer.

'I feel sick,' Serina said.

'That makes two of us,' Nicolas said. 'But we have to try to stay calm, Serina.'

'Yes, that's what Greg used to say.'

'Sounds like a sensible man. Now what else would he have advised in this situation?'

'He'd say to ring the local bushfire brigade. Find out exactly where the fire is. Now why didn't I think of that earlier?'

'Do you have their number?'

'Yes. Greg used to be president, remember?'

'Then hop to it.'

The fire was in the state forest, she was advised, but not near any dwellings at this time. The wind was changeable, however, and people were advised to keep a sharp watch, and to keep in contact with the authorities for advice.

'We'll still go and get Felicity,' Nicolas said.

'We certainly will,' Serina agreed.

'Try ringing Kirsty's mother again,' Nicolas advised.

This time Janine answered.

'Oh, Janine! I'm so relieved. I tried ringing earlier but there wasn't any answer.'

'I was outside, looking for the girls.'

That sick feeling came rushing back into Serina's stomach.

'And did you find them?'

'No, I didn't. I made them promise not to go into the forest today but you know those two. They have minds of their own.'

'But isn't there a bushfire out your way?'

'Yes. That's why I went to find them. Ken's just phoned me to tell me to be ready to leave at a moment's notice. He's been out helping fight the fire all morning. He said there wasn't any imminent danger, but in this weather he didn't want us to take any chances. I was just about to call you when you rang me.'

'I'm on my way to your place now.'

'Look, I'm sure the girls will be back any minute. They wouldn't want to stay out long in this heat.'

'You don't think they could be lost?'

'Heavens, no. They know that place like the back of their hands. Besides, all the walking tracks are well marked.'

'I tried to ring Felicity on her mobile but there was no answer. Does Kirsty have her mobile with her?'

'I'm afraid not. I found it lying on her bed.'

'Darn. We'll be another fifteen minutes getting to your place, Janine. We're coming from Port Macquarie.'

'Who's we?'

'Me and Nicolas Dupre.'

'Oh…I see.'

Serina doubted it.

'You have my mobile number, don't you?'

'Yes.'

'I won't ring anyone. Call me the moment they get back.'

Serina hung up on a deep shuddering sigh.

'Where have the little devils gone?' Nicolas demanded to know straight away.

'Into the forest.'

He swore. Then swore again, banging the steering wheel at the same time. 'I'm going to strangle that girl.'

'You'll have to get in line,' Serina quipped.

They both laughed but they were just fear-covering laughs. They quickly fell silent, Nicolas putting his foot down every chance he got. Soon Wauchope was behind them, then Rocky Creek. Serina kept staring at her mobile, which she was gripping tightly in her lap, but it didn't ring. With each passing minute, her fear increased, horrible thoughts entering her head. She could not bear it if she lost Felicity. It would be the end of her.

'This is one hell of a road,' Nicolas said as the SUV hit another pothole.

'It's not the best.'

'Much farther?'

'A couple more corners. Slow down. Their driveway is coming up on the left. There! Between those two gum trees.'

'Hell on earth,' Nicolas grumbled as he drove up the gravel road to the house that, though perched on a cleared rise, was virtually surrounded by trees. 'These places are disasters waiting to happen. Why haven't they cleared the trees farther back from the house?'

'They're not allowed to cut down any natives without permission from the local council. And getting permission is a minefield of red tape.'

'Insanity!'

'I agree. But Janine's place is safer than most. Ken's cleared out all the immediate scrub and undergrowth, which is where bushfires get their fuel. They also have sprinklers built into the roof and a fireproof cellar. Oh, look, there's Janine on the verandah. She doesn't look too happy. The girls can't have come back yet.'

Nicolas pulled the vehicle to a rather ragged halt in front of the steps and they both jumped out. The heat and wind by then was atrocious, and the thick smell of smoke on the air very worrying. So was the big black cloud on the horizon above the treetops.

'No sign of the girls yet?' a worried Serina said as she hurried towards Janine.

'Not yet. I…'

'Mum—Mum!'

Both women turned in the direction of the girl's voice. It was Kirsty, running like mad across the wide front lawn.

'Where's Felicity?' Serina demanded to know immediately.

'She's still in there,' Kirsty said, pointing back towards the forest. 'We were on our way back when we heard this crying sound not far from the track. It was a fox who'd fallen down a rabbit hole and broken its leg. We tried to get it out but it was in a right panic and slipped farther down into the hole. I told Fliss to leave it. I could tell that the fire was getting closer. But she wouldn't. You know what she's like, Mrs Harmon.'

'Yes,' Serina said with a groan.

'I didn't know what to do, Mum,' Kirsty said, a sob catching in her throat. 'I...I couldn't make her leave so I thought I'd come and get help.'

Nicolas looked at the way the fire was leaping from treetop to treetop on a nearby hilltop and realised there was no time to lose. 'Can you show me where she is, Kirsty?'

'My daughter's not going back in there!' Janine said, and hugged her child to her side.

'We don't expect her to,' Nicolas said. 'We just need to know which way to go.'

'Please, Kirsty,' Serina begged.

'It's all right, Mum,' Kirsty said, getting control of herself. 'I'll show them. She's not all that far in.'

'In that case, I'm coming, too,' Janine said.

They all ran towards the forest and the fire.

'Along here,' Kirsty said, and dived into the forest, with everyone in hot pursuit.

Despite following a well-trodden walking track, Nicolas was astonished at how quickly the forest seemed to close in around them, blocking out the light. Of course it didn't help that the sky above was filling with black smoke. Get off this trail, however, and you'd be lost in seconds.

Lost and cooked.

Nicolas had not forgotten how it had felt, being burned. Yet he didn't feel afraid for himself. His fear was all for his daughter.

'She's just in there,' Kirsty said, stopping and pointing through some thick bush on her left. 'Fliss, are you there?' she yelled out.

'Yeah,' Felicity yelled back. 'This bloody fox is stuck. Come and help me, will you?'

'I'm going to kill her,' Serina said, and was about to launch towards her daughter's voice, when Nicolas grabbed her arm.

'You go back to the house. I'll get her.'

Serina set rebellious eyes upon him.

'Take her back, Janine,' Nicolas snapped before she could say a word. 'Now!'

They all heard it then. The sound of the flames, roaring towards them.

'No!' Serina screamed, and wrenched out of Nicolas's hold. 'I won't go back without Felicity. I won't!' And she plunged into the forest, calling out to her daughter.

'You go back!' Nicolas screamed to Janine and Kirsty as he raced after her. 'I'll get them. Don't worry.'

And he would, he vowed. No way was his family going to die here today. No way!

He found them both quite quickly, Serina trying to pull her stubborn daughter away from the rabbit hole and the fox she was insanely intent on saving. Even in that short time, the intensity of the heat had grown. Nicolas couldn't see the fire yet, but he could feel it coming.

'Felicity,' he said firmly. 'You have to come with us now, or we'll all die.'

Felicity lifted startled eyes at his voice. 'Oh, it's you, Nicolas. Look, maybe you can get the fox out. You have longer arms than me.'

'Leave the damned fox, girl!'

Felicity speared him with a mutinous look. 'I will not leave the damned fox!'

'Felicity! For pity's sake!' Serina screamed at her daughter. 'Just do what your father says!'

Nicolas gaped at Serina's immediately stricken face, then at Felicity, who looked more than a little confused.

'Silly woman,' Nicolas said straight away. 'Doesn't know if she's Arthur or Martha at the moment. It's Nicolas here, Serina, not Greg. Still, it's a shame Greg isn't here, given his wealth of experience with bushfires. So tell me, Felicity, what would your dad have done at this moment?'

'He'd have saved my fox if I'd asked him to,'

she replied, her eyes suddenly filling with tears. 'But he's not here, is he? He's dead.'

'That's true,' Nicolas agreed. 'But I think he'd save his lovely daughter, too, wouldn't he? So let's get your fox out of that hole and get us all safely out of this forest.'

The fox wouldn't cooperate. Pain and fear were making it panic. Nicolas lifted it out of the hole in the end, though not before the animal had bitten him on the hand.

Not that he cared. Nothing mattered but getting the people he loved to safety.

When Felicity hesitated to leave again, he glared at her. 'What now?' he demanded to know.

'My mobile phone. It's at the bottom of the rabbit hole.'

Nicolas almost swore. Instead, he gritted his teeth and prayed for patience. 'I'll buy you another phone,' he said. 'A better one. Now go, girl. And take your mother with you,' he said, only then noticing that Serina was still standing there in a shocked silence.

This time Felicity did as she was told, grabbing her mother's arm and pulling her towards the trail, Nicolas hot on their heels carrying the fox.

Not that they were out of the woods yet. The

winds had whipped the fire into a fireball that was moving at tremendous speed towards them through the bush.

'Run,' he screamed at Felicity and Serina. 'Run faster.'

They made it, just, bursting out onto clear ground with the flames licking at their heels. Even so, they didn't stop running till they reached the house where Janine and Kirsty were waiting for them with anxiety on their faces.

'I'm so glad you're all right,' Janine said, then shot Nicolas a rueful glance. 'I see you brought the fox.'

Nicolas shrugged. 'Felicity wouldn't leave it behind.'

'He was wonderful,' Felicity said. 'Here, Nicolas. I'll take the fox now. I know what to do with it. Kirsty and I have a makeshift hospital in one of the sheds.'

'Excuse me, missy,' Janine said firmly, nodding towards where the fire had reached the grassy surrounds of the property. 'But we're all going down to the cellar till this fire is under control. Ken's just rung. He said they're on their way here and they're bringing a couple of water-bombing helicopters, but he doesn't want us taking any chances. My husband's one of the volunteer firefighters,' she explained to Nicolas.

'Well, the fox comes, too,' Felicity insisted. 'Kirsty, we'll need a beach towel to wrap her up in. And a dish of water for her to have a drink. She'll be very thirsty.'

'We're all pretty thirsty,' Nicolas said, and wrapped a tender arm around Serina. 'Aren't we, sweetheart?'

'What?' she asked, her voice somewhat vague. Still in shock, he realised.

'I said we're all thirsty.'

'Oh. Yes, I suppose so.'

'There are drinks down in the cellar,' Janine informed him. 'And a cupboard full of food. But no toilet. So anyone who wants to use the bathroom had better do so now. We might be down there for a while.'

No one did. Possibly because they were all dehydrated.

It was a large cellar, with a wine rack along one wall, an old sofa along another, boxes and bits and pieces stacked along another and several chairs around a table in the centre. Temperature wise, it was lovely and cool.

Nicolas pulled out a chair for Serina at the

table whilst Janine got some cans of drink from an ancient bar fridge. Felicity sat next to Kirsty on the sofa with the towel-wrapped fox in her lap, stroking its ears and singing some kind of song. There was not a peep out of the mesmerised animal.

'I've spawned Doctor Doolittle,' Nicolas muttered under his breath when Janine moved away to give Kirsty and Felicity their cans of Coke.

'Hush up,' Serina said sharply.

Nicolas sighed. 'Serina, you don't have to worry. No one heard me and I covered your earlier blunder.'

'But what if you hadn't been able to? What if Felicity had guessed the truth?'

'She didn't.'

Serina just shook her head. 'You just don't understand, do you?'

Janine came back to sit at their table and Nicolas lifted his can of drink to his mouth.

Janine gasped. 'Nicolas! Did you know your hand was bleeding?'

'What? Show me!' Serina said.

'It's nothing much. The fox bit me.'

'There's a first-aid kit here somewhere,' Janine said, and went in search of it.

'What kind of person am I?' Serina said bleakly. 'I didn't notice that you were bleeding. And I haven't even thanked you for what you did out there. I'm a terrible person.' And she burst into tears.

'What's wrong with Mum?' Felicity asked straight away, her voice worried.

'She's just in shock,' Nicolas replied as he held a weeping Serina against him with his non-bleeding hand. 'You must realise how worried she was, Felicity. She thought that you were going to die, too. Like your dad.'

'Oh… Oh I see.'

'I hope so, Felicity,' Nicolas said firmly. 'Next time, think before you risk your life. Your mother needs you just as much as that fox.'

'Found the first-aid kit!' Janine piped up.

'What do you need the first-aid kit for?' Felicity asked.

'Nicolas's hand is bleeding. Your fox bit him.'

'Your good hand or your bad hand?' she asked him.

'My bad hand,' he replied.

'Oh, that's all right then.'

He laughed whilst Serina wept on. If it hadn't have been funny he might have cried, too.

Nicolas's hand had been properly attended to and Serina had stopped crying when suddenly, there were sounds overhead and all eyes simultaneously went upwards. The cellar door was flung open and daylight flooded down the steps. Fortunately, there was no smell of smoke, and no other evidence of the fire having reached the house.

'Everyone okay down here?' called a deep male voice.

'Yes, Ken,' Janine said, jumping up onto her feet and racing over to the bottom of the cellar staircase. 'How's the house?'

'Right as rain.' Ken, a big brawny guy dressed in his yellow firefighting suit and holding a hard hat, came down the steps. 'The wind changed again and sent the fire back in the direction it came from, which was a bonus. So!' He smiled broadly as he gathered his wife into his arms then glanced over at Felicity and Kirsty. 'I see our own little rescue team has been busy. What do you have this time, girls?'

'A fox,' Kirsty said as both girls struggled to their feet. 'It has a broken leg.'

'We'll have to take it to the vet,' Felicity said, and looked straight at Nicolas.

He was taken aback. Why look at him? Why not Ken, or her mother?

'Dad always took all my sick and injured animals to the vet for me,' she said, her voice just a little shaky.

Nicolas's heart turned over.

'You'll have to give me directions,' he said. 'I have no idea where the nearest vet is.'

'I'll show you,' Felicity exclaimed, her pretty face breaking into a smile….

CHAPTER TWENTY-ONE

'I HOPE the fox will be okay,' Nicolas said.

He was sitting with Serina in the vet's waiting room, Felicity having taken her patient into the consulting room fifteen minutes earlier. Although the hospital wasn't open for surgery for another hour, there'd been a bell on the front door to ring for emergencies, and luckily the vet—who lived at the back of the building—had been at home.

'I'm sure it'll be fine,' Serina replied. 'Ted's a good vet.'

'Let's hope so. Felicity's somewhat obsessive about saving wildlife, isn't she?'

'Mmmm.'

'Do you think she has any idea of the risks she took today?'

'I doubt it.'

'She needs a firm hand, Serina, and a protective one.'

'I do my best, Nicolas.'

'She needs a father.'

Serina gave him a panicky look. 'You promised you would never tell her.'

'And I won't. But how about a stepfather?'

'Stepfather?' Serina echoed, her eyes blinking wide.

'Yes, Serina, stepfather. I was going to wait till tonight to propose to you over a candlelit dinner with a big diamond ring in my pocket. But I doubt you'll come out with me tonight after what happened today. I also doubt that a big diamond ring would impress you, anyway. So I'm asking you now—will you marry me?'

Serina just kept on staring at him.

Nicolas sighed. 'I can guess what you're going to say,' he went on before she could argue with him. 'We come from different worlds. We don't really know each other anymore. We've left it too late. Well I have the perfect answer for all of that and it's balderdash! All that matters is that we love each other. We've always loved each other. If there's anything that today should have shown you, it's that all life is a risk. We could have fried in there today. All three of us. Instead we're alive and well. Look, I promise you that I won't ask anything of you that would make you unhappy. I won't ask you to move, or change, or anything. We can make this work, Serina. I'll make it work. Trust me, darling, and just say yes.'

Serina closed her eyes for a long moment. When she opened them again, they were awash with tears.

Nicolas thought they were tears of happiness.

But hc was wrong.

'Oh, Nicolas…if only you'd asked me to marry you twenty years ago. Or that night at the Opera House. Or even yesterday. Yesterday, I might still have said yes. Though of course that would have still been a big mistake. What happened today showed me that I can't marry you. Ever. Neither can I have a relationship with you. Not one around here, anyway.'

'What? But why?'

'Because I couldn't bear it.'

'Couldn't bear being what?'

'Couldn't bear keeping another secret. Couldn't bear being afraid all the time of the truth coming out. It was bad enough when I was married to Greg. I coped because I was the only one who knew. And because you were another world away. I nearly died today when I said what I said. I felt ill. I still feel ill, thinking about it. Because if Felicity ever found out Greg wasn't her real father, she'd never forgive me. She'd hate me. Yes, life is a risk, but I can't risk that, Nicolas, no matter how much I love you. I'm sorry.'

Nicolas just sat there. Stunned, hurt, devastated.

He struggled to find the right words to say. The right questions to ask.

'When you said you can't have a relationship with me around here, what exactly did you mean?'

'You know very well what I meant, Nicolas. I'll visit you overseas every now and then, but I don't want you coming here. Not anymore. Because one day, one of us might say something in front of Felicity—or someone else—like we did today.'

Nicolas's head understood her reasoning. But his heart reacted very badly. 'I offer you marriage,' he said, bitter resentment in his voice, 'and that's what you offer me in return? Well I'm sorry, too, Serina, but a dirty weekend here and there is not enough for me. I love you and I want to spend quality time with you. I also love my daughter. That's something I discovered today. I would never do anything to hurt her. I gave you my word that I would never tell her I was her father, and I will keep my word. But I want to be able to play some kind of role in her upbringing. I want to watch her grow up. I want to watch over her. It seems, however, that you're going to deny me even that.'

'Nicolas, I…I…'

'Please don't say another word,' he snapped. 'The subject is now closed. We are now closed. Finito.' He made a chopping gesture across his throat as he stood up. 'I will wait outside for you. Then, when Felicity is finished, I will drive you both home and say my goodbyes with our daughter present. That way I can be assured that I will not say anything further that I might later regret. No, Serina,' he snarled when she opened her mouth again. 'Do not waste your breath. I have always been a very black-and-white person. You don't love me the way I love you. You never have. So please, let's just leave it at that.' And whirling, he stalked out of the waiting room.

Serina stared after him, her head whirling, but her heart like lead in her chest. *He doesn't mean it,* she reasoned. *He's just angry with me. He can't mean it.*

But he did mean it, she was to discover to her despair. He'd meant every word.

He drove them home and said his goodbyes, Felicity quite upset by his decision to leave Port Macquarie the following day.

'But I was hoping you'd be with us for Christmas,' she said plaintively. 'Mum, tell him he has to stay.'

Serina just shook her head. She could already see that Nicolas was not about to change his mind. And she couldn't trust herself to speak.

'I have to go, Felicity,' he said, and gave his daughter a quick hug. 'I'm needed back in New York. The show must go on, sweetheart. Look after your mother for me. And give my regards to Mrs Johnson.'

Felicity waved him off from the front porch, her goodbye smile fading once he was gone.

'I don't see why he had to go back to New York in such a hurry,' she grumbled whilst Serina set about feeding a noisily complaining Midnight. 'Unless, of course, he does have a girlfriend back there. Did you ever ask him, Mum, if he was dating that Japanese violinist?'

'Yes.'

'And?'

'He said he wasn't.'

'I didn't think so. Kirsty and I reckon he's still in love with you.'

'What makes you think that?'

'The way he kept looking at you.'

'What way is that?'

'Like he adored the ground you walked on.'

Serina swallowed the great lump in her throat, then forced out a small laugh. 'You two girls. You're just like Allie and Emma, incorrigible romantics. If he adored the ground I walked on then what's he doing going back to New York? Look, could you put this cat food away for me, love? I have to go to the bathroom.'

She just made it into the bathroom before the tears came.

It was not the first time she was to cry uncontrollably during the following few days.

She cried when the mobile phone arrived for Felicity, posted from Sydney airport. Then again when she had to go into Port Macquarie to buy Christmas presents. And again when she passed the spot where Nicolas had pulled the SUV off the road and kissed her.

She dreaded Christmas, fearing she would not get through the day without breaking down, especially since that year they were holding their family celebrations at the Harmons, in the house where Nicolas had lived. Serina managed to keep it together till Felicity's grandparents requested Felicity do an encore of the medley she'd played at the talent quest…on Nicolas's old piano, no less.

Serina started weeping shortly after her daughter started playing and she just couldn't stop.

Fortunately, Greg's parents didn't connect her distress with Nicolas. They thought she was still grieving for their son.

In the end, Serina had to go home where a very upset Felicity demanded to know what the matter was.

'It's Nicolas, isn't it?' she said when Serina didn't enlighten her. 'He's broken your heart again like Grandma said he did once before. You still love him, don't you?'

Serina just couldn't bring herself to lie.

'Yes,' she confessed brokenly. 'Yes, I still love him.'

'But he doesn't love you?'

'Oh, yes, yes, he does. Very much.'

'Then why did he go back to New York?'

Serina looked deep into her daughter's eyes.

'Because I asked him to go,' she admitted.

'Mum! But why?'

'Because I was afraid…'

'Afraid of what?'

Serina's face twisted, her courage failing her once more. 'I can't tell you.'

'Of course you can, Mum. You always say that we can tell each other anything!'

'If I tell you, you might hate me.'

'I would never hate you, Mum. You are the best mother in the whole wide world.'

'Oh. Oh, dear…'

'Mum,' Felicity said firmly. 'You have to tell me what's making you so unhappy and we'll work it out together.'

Could she really tell her? Dared she?

Serina thought of Nicolas, all alone in New York and wanting so much to be a part of their lives. And then she thought of herself, living the rest of her life the way she'd felt this past week. Not just lonely, but horribly guilty. More guilty than she'd ever felt when she'd been married to Greg.

No more guilt, she decided. No more secrets. Serina said a little prayer first, then started talking….

CHAPTER TWENTY-TWO

THE snow had stopped falling by the time Nicolas alighted the cab outside his apartment block, but the air was bitterly cold.

'Don't know how you stand it, Mike,' he said to his favourite doorman as he hurried up the front steps.

'I'm used to it, Mr Dupre. But then I'm a New Yorker. Not an Aussie like you. Better get yourself inside now, before you catch your death.'

An Aussie, Nicolas was thinking as he stepped into the invitingly warm lobby. He'd actually stopped thinking of himself as Australian. Till his recent return to the country of his birth.

Now he couldn't stop thinking about the place. And the daughter he had there. The daughter he would never see again.

He'd once loved Christmas in New York. He'd even loved the cold. This year he'd hated it all. He'd wanted to be back there in Rocky Creek, with Serina and Felicity. He'd wanted to shower them both with gifts. Wanted to kiss them and hug them and just…be with them.

Instead, he'd spent the day, alone, in his apartment, having refused several last-minute invitations to Christmas dinner. He hadn't even bought any presents, though he did give his usual cash gifts to Mike and Chad. He spent Boxing Day alone as well, and the twenty-seventh.

Today, he'd forced himself to go out. He'd attended the matinee show of a play that had just opened—and he found deadly dull—after which he'd had a bite to eat before heading home. What he would do tomorrow he had no idea. Go jogging in the park, maybe… Something that would put a bit of life back into him.

Because he felt dead. Dead inside.

I should never have cut Serina out of my life like that, he realised grimly. *Being bloody black-and-white was a recipe for depression of the worst kind.*

'Mr Dupre!' Chad called out to him as he made his way with his head down across the lobby.

Nicolas took a deep breath as he ground to a halt. *Don't take it out on the lad,* he lectured himself. *It's not his fault that you want to strangle him, just for talking to you.*

He tried not to scowl as he turned back in the direction of the reception desk. 'Yes, Chad?'

'There's another pink letter for you. From Australia.'

'What?'

A stunned Nicolas hurried over to the desk where Chad was indeed holding out a bright pink envelope to him. It was exactly the same as the last one. Though there were several important differences. There was nothing written on it except his name.

He flipped it over. Nothing on the other side as well.

'I don't get it,' he said, totally thrown. 'How did you know this was from Australia? There's no stamp on it or any sender's name and address. In fact, there's no damned address on the front, either. So how on earth did it even get here?'

Chad looked a little sheepish. But not too worried. 'It was…um…hand-delivered.'

'Hand-delivered?'

'Yes,' a woman's voice said behind him. 'By me.'

Nicolas's chest tightened. Dear God, he knew that voice.

He whirled and there she was: his Serina.

'Felicity sent me,' she said simply as she walked slowly towards him from the lobby's lounge area. 'That's from her.' And she nodded towards the pink envelope.

'I don't understand….' And he didn't. But the beginning of a wonderful hope was clawing its way into his, till then, dead heart.

Serina glanced over his shoulder at Chad, who, no doubt, could overhear their conversation.

'Come over here,' she said quietly, and drew him towards a lounge in a far corner of the lobby, next to which sat a small suitcase and a very large handbag.

Nicolas's heart was pounding in his chest by the time they were sitting down together.

'Tell me what's going on, for pity's sake!'

'I told Felicity the truth, Nicolas. I told her you were her father.'

Nicolas literally stopped breathing at this astonishing piece of news. 'And?' he choked out.

Her smile would have melted the arctic. 'She didn't hate me.'

'What…what about me?' Never in his life had Nicolas stammered the way he did at that moment.

'Oh, Nicolas, how could she possibly hate you? None of it was your fault. The guilt was all mine.'

'That's not true, my darling,' he said as he took her hands in his.

'Oh, yes it is. Please, Nicolas, let me own my sins. I should have told you, way back then. I took the easy way out. But I paid for it and so did you. Felicity took me to task for the way I've treated you.'

'She wasn't too upset about Greg not being her real father?'

'She was very upset at first. But I made her see that Greg was her father, in every way but genetically. A wonderful father.'

'Which he was,' Nicolas agreed.

'Yes. I hope you don't mind, my darling, but neither of us want to tell anyone else the truth, especially Greg's parents. They'd be shattered.'

'Yes, they would be. I could see that.'

'They're very elderly, you know. There will come a day in the not too distant future when it won't matter so much who knows the truth.'

'I don't mind other people not knowing,' he said, 'as long as my daughter knows.'

'She asked me to ask you to open that letter in front of me.'

'Did she now?' He ripped open the pink envelope with some trepidation. The letter was computer-generated as before.

Dear Nicolas

Sorry, but I don't feel right calling you Dad. I already have a dad. But I think it's kinda cool that you are my father. No wonder I play the piano a bit like you. Anyway I'm glad Mum told me the truth, because I reckon I might have figured it out some day. Now look, Nicolas, it's Mum I'm really writing to you about. She's been very sad since you left. I mean seriously seriously sad. She still loves you and she says you still love her. Which I sure hope is true, because if it's not, I will never speak to you again as long as I live. Which would be a tragedy of the highest order as I like you heaps. So please please ask her to marry you again. And come back to Australia to live.

Bye for now,

Your secret daughter,

Felicity Harmon.

PS. Please email me the very second Mum says yes. (Which she will.)

PPS. I'd like a baby brother or sister please. ASAP.
PPS. I still don't want to become a concert pianist.

Nicolas couldn't help laughing.

'What is it?' Serina demanded to know. 'What did she say?'

He just handed her the letter.

Serina groaned. 'Oh, dear. She is terribly precocious, isn't she?'

'I think she's marvellous,' Nicolas said.

'She's the one who found out your actual address. From that program you did on television a few years ago. She got the phone number somehow as well and rang the desk to make sure you were staying here and not in London before she booked my flights. She insisted I come in person. She said it would be cowardly of me to just email, or ring.'

'You're no coward. I think you are the bravest lady I've ever met. So will you marry me, my darling?'

'Need you ask?'

'Had to. Or my daughter said she wouldn't speak to me for the rest of her life.'

'Then yes, Nicolas. I'll marry you.'

He smiled then hugged her. 'So what do you think about her other request for a baby brother or sister, ASAP?'

Serina's eyes sparkled. 'I'm willing, if you're willing.'

'In that case I think we'll go upstairs and get started on that project straight away. But first... Chad!' he called out across the lobby as he stood up. 'Am I right in assuming you and Serina are already acquainted?'

'Er...yes, Mr Dupre. We had quite a long chat earlier on. That's how I knew she was from Australia. Though I already guessed, from her accent.'

'We're getting married, Chad.'

'That's wonderful news, Mr Dupre. Mike will be thrilled. He's been a bit worried about you. I'll go tell him right away.'

'You do that. Now we've got something we've got to do straight away,' he said to Serina as he picked up her luggage.

'Yes, I know,' she said, standing up, too. 'The email.'

'The email can wait. I can't. Come on.'

They reached the lifts, where Nicolas was

about to press the up button, when Serina stopped him. 'There's something I want to say first.'

'Do you have to?'

'Yes. I want to say that I love you, Nicolas Dupre. I've never stopped loving you. When I was a young girl, before you even noticed me, I used to dream that one day we would get married, and have a family together. And now that dream is going to come true. Thank you, Nicolas. For still loving me. And for asking me to marry me again. Thank you.'

Nicolas couldn't speak for a long moment.

He dropped the luggage and reached out to curve his hands over her shoulders.

'It's I who should be thanking you,' he said, his voice husky. 'For still loving me, after all these years. Do you remember my saying that there was a woman once whom I wanted to marry but it didn't work out?'

Serina nodded.

'You were that woman, my love. You. Never anyone else.'

'Oh, Nicolas…'

'No. No more tears. From now on we're not going to look back. Our new life together is just beginning. We're going to be the happiest couple to ever live in Rocky Creek.'

Serina's eyes widened. 'Rocky Creek?'

'Yes, damn it. Rocky Creek. If we're going to have more children, I can't really drag them all over the world all the time, can I?'

'But you won't be happy living in Rocky Creek all the time!' Serina protested.

'Who said?'

'You said.'

'True. Okay, I'll buy that penthouse in Port Macquarie and do a bit of commuting. That sound feasible enough for you?'

'Very feasible. Felicity wants to go to school in Port Macquarie next year. They've not long opened a new high school there. It has a great reputation already. It is rather expensive. But she said you could afford it.'

'What? That girl! She's incorrigible!'

'Indeed. I wonder where she gets her ruthlessness from?'

'Hey, don't blame me for everything. She has half your genes, you know.'

'You didn't say that about her piano playing! You claimed all those genes.'

Suddenly, Nicolas grinned. 'We're arguing over our kid already.'

'Parents always argue over their children.'

'Do they? I rather like it.'

'You won't once the boys start calling. Which will be any day now.'

Serina almost laughed at Nicolas's horrified expression. 'She's not old enough for boys.'

'She'll be thirteen next year. In two years she'll be fifteen. I was fifteen when I went to your graduation.'

'My God. Where is she now? Who's she staying with whilst you're over here?'

'Kirsty's parents.'

'What? She's back out there in bushfire land?'

'We can't mollycoddle her, Nicolas.'

'Oh, yes I can. I'm her father. I can mollycoddle her all I like! You're going home, Serina, and I'm coming with you.'

'Really, Nicolas, are you quite sure about that?' And sliding her arms up around his neck, she kissed him.

They didn't fly home till after the New Year.

EPILOGUE

Christmas Day, one year later...

NICOLAS sat at the head of the huge dining table, with Serina on his right, and three-month-old Sebastian lying in his bouncinette between them.

'How about a toast, everyone?' Nicolas said, and lifted his wineglass high.

There were eight other people seated around the table. Ken, Janine and Kirsty; Bert and Franny; Margaret, Serina's mother; Mrs Johnson; and of course, Felicity.

This was what a Christmas should be, Nicolas realised. Not presents so much—though he had gone over the top a bit this first year—but friends and family all gathered together.

'Happy Christmas!' he said, and clicked his wineglass against Serina's.

'Happy Christmas!' everyone chorused.

Sebastian responded to the noise by rocking madly back and forth in his bouncinette, flapping his arms and laughing his highly infectious laugh.

Everyone laughed with him, then got on with eating. Everyone except Serina, who wanted to take a moment to drink in, not the wine, but her happiness.

What a year it had been! So much had happened, everything orchestrated by Nicolas with speed and efficiency. They'd married by special licence in the middle of January, at the old Rocky Creek church, then honeymooned in both New York and London, during which both Nicolas's properties were sold. By the time they returned home to Australia in early February, Serina was well and truly pregnant. She'd actually fallen during the first week she'd spent with Nicolas in New York but kept that news to herself for a while.

On returning to Australia, Nicolas decided that the penthouse apartment—which he'd put a deposit on—wasn't suitable for family living. So he pulled out of that contract, then took Serina and Felicity house-hunting. They ended up buying, not just a house, but a small acreage not far from the Port Macquarie racecourse. It had belonged to a horse trainer who'd decided to go farther north.

Both Felicity and Serina had fallen in love with the place at first sight, Felicity because of the stables—extremely suitable to house sick animals in!—and Serina because of the house, which, though only five years old, was in the design of a colonial farmhouse with a high pitched roof and verandahs all around. Although much larger, it reminded her of the house she'd been brought up in and where she'd always been very happy.

And it was from this new and much-loved home that Nicolas had driven her to the hospital to have their baby.

Her pregnancy was the only worry that this year had brought Serina. Despite being thrilled at falling so quickly, she had been secretly concerned that she might have to endure another ten-month pregnancy before popping out a clone of Felicity. The news during her four-month ultrasound that she was having a boy eased her mind somewhat, but she was still a little nervous over what her baby might look like, especially if his birth was delayed.

She need not have worried. Right on her due

date her water broke, and after a thankfully short labour, Sebastian came into the world, the spitting image of his father. Nicolas had been over the moon and everyone who came to visit oohed and aahed over the babe's angelic appearance.

Serina had anticipated that Nicolas would be besotted with his son. And he was. She hadn't been quite so sure about Felicity's reaction. After all, Felicity had been top dog in the family for thirteen years.

But Felicity quickly became just as besotted with Sebastian as his father. She spent every spare second with her baby brother, playing with him and playing to him. On the grand piano Nicolas had bought her. She told Serina in secret one day that she knew Nicolas was disappointed that she didn't want to become a concert pianist, so she was determined to program Sebastian into fulfilling his father's wishes.

'You're not eating your dinner, Serina,' Nicolas said with a frown in his voice. 'I hope you're not on some silly diet.'

'Good heavens, no.' And she picked up her knife and fork. 'I'll be having seconds later. I love turkey.'

She'd taken several mouthfuls when Felicity suddenly stood up from where she was sitting at the other end of the table.

'I have a toast I want to make, too,' she said, and lifted her glass of Coke. 'To Nicolas. The best stepfather in the whole world.'

Serina's heart squeezed tight.

'To Nicolas,' everyone said, then drank.

'One more thing,' Felicity added. 'I've talked this over with Nanna and Pop and they think it's a good idea. The thing is…I don't want to have a different surname than my brother. So I'm going to be known as Felicity Harmon Dupre from now on. If that's all right with you, Nicolas.'

Serina saw the muscles working overtime in Nicolas's throat.

'Absolutely all right,' he finally managed to say.

'And you, Mum? You don't mind?'

'Not at all, darling. I think it's an excellent idea.'

'What a lucky girl you are, Felicity,' Serina's mother said as Felicity sat down. 'To have been blessed with two wonderful fathers.'

'Felicity is a lucky girl,' Nicolas told Serina as

they lay in each other's arms that night, their son asleep in the cot next to their bed. 'But no one is more blessed than me. I have everything any man could ever want.'

Serina glanced up from where she was snuggled against his bare chest. 'You don't miss show business?'

'Not at the moment. But if I ever do, I can always buy a place in Sydney and get back into it. This is all I want to do right now. Spend every day with you and my children.'

'You'll eventually get bored.'

'Maybe. Meanwhile, what say we make another baby?'

Serina's breath caught. 'So soon?'

'The sooner the better. I didn't realise how much I would enjoy having a baby. The last three months have been the best three months of my life.'

'You might change your mind once Sebastian learns to walk. And talk. Haven't you heard of the terrible twos?'

'All the more reason to start a baby straight away, before I get disillusioned.'

'But if I have another baby I might have to give up work.'

'What a good idea! Then you can stay home all day every day with yours truly.'

'You are a wickedly selfish man.'

'It is a failing of mine. But you love me, just the same.'

'I don't know why.'

He showed her why.

Then he showed her again, just to be sure.

AUTHOR'S NOTE

Some of you may have read that I was born in Port Macquarie. So you will know already that Port is a real seaside town, on the mid North Coast of New South Wales, Australia. Wauchope—pronounced Warhope—is also a real town. Rocky Creek, however, is a place of my imagination.

For the first ten years of my life I lived on Rawdon Island, which is in the middle of the Hastings River, between Port Macquarie and Wauchope. My father was the school teacher there, my mother a dressmaker. Every Thursday we went to Wauchope to shop, and every Saturday to Port Macquarie, where my parents played golf and my two brothers, my sister and myself went to the movies. That was where my love of story began.

I recently revisited Port Macquarie to see what it was like nowadays. Yes, the old picture theatre is still there. And so is an old house with steep terraced lawns where I used to roll down whilst my mother was inside, doing dress fittings with the lady owner. There is no apartment block called Blue Horizons. At least, not one like mine. But it is real in my mind, as are my characters and their wonderful love story. Very real. Hopefully, they are now real in yours.

MILLS & BOON PUBLISH EIGHT LARGE PRINT TITLES A MONTH. THESE ARE THE EIGHT TITLES FOR NOVEMBER 2010.

❧

A NIGHT, A SECRET...A CHILD
Miranda Lee

HIS UNTAMED INNOCENT
Sara Craven

THE GREEK'S PREGNANT LOVER
Lucy Monroe

THE MÉLENDEZ FORGOTTEN MARRIAGE
Melanie Milburne

AUSTRALIA'S MOST ELIGIBLE BACHELOR
Margaret Way

THE BRIDESMAID'S SECRET
Fiona Harper

CINDERELLA: HIRED BY THE PRINCE
Marion Lennox

THE SHEIKH'S DESTINY
Melissa James

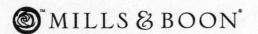

MILLS & BOON PUBLISH EIGHT LARGE PRINT TITLES A MONTH. THESE ARE THE EIGHT TITLES FOR DECEMBER 2010.

❧

THE PREGNANCY SHOCK
Lynne Graham

FALCO: THE DARK GUARDIAN
Sandra Marton

ONE NIGHT...NINE-MONTH SCANDAL
Sarah Morgan

THE LAST KOLOVSKY PLAYBOY
Carol Marinelli

DOORSTEP TWINS
Rebecca Winters

THE COWBOY'S ADOPTED DAUGHTER
Patricia Thayer

SOS: CONVENIENT HUSBAND REQUIRED
Liz Fielding

WINNING A GROOM IN 10 DATES
Cara Colter